LIZZIE AND
GO AWAY FOR T.

Dyan Sheldon is a children's writer, adult
novelist and humorist. Her children's titles
include the award-winning *The Whales' Song*,
as well as *Lizzie and Charley Go Shopping*;
Lizzie and Charley Go to the Movies; *Leon
Loves Bugs*; *Undercover Angel*; *Undercover
Angel Strikes Again*; and *He's Not My Dog*.
Among her numerous titles for young adults
are *Confessions of a Teenage Drama Queen*;
My Perfect Life; *Planet Janet*; *The Boy of My
Dreams*; and *Tall, Thin and Blonde*.

Books by the same author

Elena the Frog
He's Not My Dog
Leon Loves Bugs
Lizzie and Charley Go Shopping
Lizzie and Charley Go to the Movies

For older readers

Undercover Angel
Undercover Angel Strikes Again
The Boy of My Dreams
Confessions of a Teenage Drama Queen
My Perfect Life
Ride On, Sister Vincent
Tall, Thin and Blonde
And Baby Makes Two
Planet Janet

DYAN SHELDON

WALKER BOOKS
AND SUBSIDIARIES
LONDON • BOSTON • SYDNEY

First published 2002 by Walker Books Ltd
87 Vauxhall Walk, London SE11 5HJ

2 4 6 8 10 9 7 5 3 1

Text © 2002 Dyan Sheldon
Cover illustration © 2002 Nick Sharratt

The right of Dyan Sheldon to be identified as author of
this work has been asserted by her in accordance with
the Copyright, Designs and Patents Act 1988

This book has been typeset in Plantin

Printed in Great Britain by Cox & Wyman Ltd, Reading, Berkshire

British Library Cataloguing in Publication Data:
a catalogue record for this book
is available from the British Library

ISBN 0-7445-9075-2

For Rocky and Kev

Contents

Mrs Moscos and Lizzie Have Another Difference of Opinion

One sunny Friday afternoon, Lizzie Wesson stepped out of her house, dragging an enormous pink bag by its bright green straps. The front door banged shut behind her. Lizzie was happy as she dragged the pink bag down the steps and along the path to the street. As Lizzie neared the gate, the hedge that stood between the Wessons' and the house next door suddenly spoke.

"And where are you off to on this beautiful day, Lizzie Wesson?" it wanted to know. "Will you be crossing the Rocky Mountains on a mule? Journeying through the desert on top of a camel? Sailing the Indian Ocean in a barquentine?"

"Charley and I are going away for the weekend with my parents," answered Lizzie. She dropped the bright green straps and leaned over the hedge.

Lizzie's neighbour, Mrs Moscos, had recently dug up her vegetable patch and built a pond in her front garden. It was a large pond, but it was crowded with so many grasses and lilies that what could be seen of the water was yellowish green. At the moment Mrs Moscos was kneeling beside the pond, planting very large ferns around its rim. The ferns made Lizzie think of a jungle. Only Mrs Moscos would plant a jungle on Meteor Drive. Everyone else had roses.

"Are you certain you're only going away for the weekend?" asked Mrs Moscos. She looked up at Lizzie. "With all of that baggage you are pulling along? I rather imagined you were going away at least for a month."

Mrs Moscos was a woman of many talents, and one of them was for making Lizzie feel defensive.

"It's only one bag," Lizzie snapped. She glanced at her bulging bag. One of the seams was starting to tear. Her new swimsuit was poking through. "And it isn't *that* big really." One bag for three whole days didn't seem like a lot to her. "We *are* staying till Monday evening."

Mrs Moscos picked up her trowel and started to dig another hole. "And just what will you be doing on this glorious weekend then – besides changing your clothes?"

Mrs Moscos claimed she came from somewhere in Eastern Europe and was very peculiar. Indeed, it was Lizzie's opinion that Mrs Moscos was one of the most peculiar people in the world. Her front garden was only one example. Mrs Moscos had very strong views on everything from shopping to going to the cinema and, on the whole, these views were the opposite of everyone else's. They were certainly the opposite of Lizzie's. Mrs Moscos never agreed with Lizzie on anything. Today, however, Lizzie was much too happy to let Mrs Moscos's oddness bother her. She reached into her pocket and pulled out a crumpled brochure.

"This is where we're going." Lizzie held the crumpled brochure over the hedge to Mrs Moscos. On the front was a photograph of an enormous, very modern building and several smaller buildings surrounded by acres of fields and woods. Across the top of the photograph, in very large letters, it said:

WELCOME TO PARK WORLD

Underneath that it said:

A PLACE OF FUN AND ADVENTURE FOR THE WHOLE FAMILY – WHERE THE EXTRAORDINARY IS COMMONPLACE.

Mrs Moscos seemed to be a lot less interested in the brochure than she was in the dirt she was scooping out of the ground, but she reached up one hand in a red rubber glove trimmed with feathers and took it from Lizzie. "And what's so extraordinary about that?" Mrs Moscos looked from the photograph to Lizzie. "Are you telling me that you're so excited because you're going to a hotel?"

Lizzie's voice rose indignantly. "It's not *just* a hotel, Mrs Moscos," she corrected. "It's Park World." Lizzie was an authority on Park World and all its wonders. She had read the brochure dozens of times, which explained the shocking condition it was in. *"Park World is set in an untamed wilderness,"* Lizzie explained, quoting directly from the brochure. "It has everything anyone could possibly want. Four cinemas, ice-skating, roller-blading, skateboarding, golf, games, indoor and outdoor swimming pools, water rides, tennis, ping-pong, shuffle-board, badminton, miniature golf, archery, horse-riding, a disco every night, and…" Having more or less run out of breath as well as activities, Lizzie paused. "And … well, everything. There's even a safari park near by."

"Ah," said Mrs Moscos. "A safari park. Without which, obviously, no world is complete."

"It's well cool," maintained Lizzie. "It has everything."

Mrs Moscos gave Lizzie one of her less pleasant looks. "It doesn't sound like *everything* to me," said Mrs Moscos. "To my mind, it sounds rather like a cruise liner with trees and no ocean."

Lizzie frowned. She had no idea what Mrs Moscos was on about, suddenly talking about cruise liners and oceans, but she often had no idea what Mrs Moscos was on about. "Um…" she said.

"Of course, a boat would be so much more satisfying in the long run, wouldn't it?" continued Mrs Moscos. Her eyes were on the sky. "The movement … the sense of enormity … the possibility of unexpected destinations…" She smiled at a passing cloud. "And, of course, like most people, I have always had a weakness for pirates. It can be an exciting life, and even a productive one." She smiled at another cloud. "If the circumstances are correct, that is…"

Unlike Mrs Moscos and most people, Lizzie did not have a weakness for pirates. In addition, she had no interest whatsoever in movement, senses of enormity or unexpected destinations – or, for that matter, in boats. The only boating Lizzie had ever done was in a rowing boat in the park, and she got a blister on her hand that hurt for two days.

Mrs Moscos turned back to the brochure. "I see that at least they do have sailing." She waved the Park World leaflet up and down in the air in a far from comforting way. "Imagine rolling and swaying on a windswept sea… Now that is something to look forward to."

Lizzie disagreed. The only rolling and swaying she was looking forward to was at the nightly disco, though she knew better than to mention that to Mrs Moscos.

"I doubt that we'll have time for sailing," said Lizzie diplomatically. "Because there's so much else to do."

"For example, ping-pong." Mrs Moscos shook her head sadly. "A girl your age should be reaching for the stars, not the ping-pong paddle, Lizzie Wesson." She handed back the brochure with a disappointed sigh. "You want to have some real fun while you're young and can enjoy it."

Lizzie could see that, as usual, Mrs Moscos had missed the point completely. "But Charley and I *are* going to have fun. We're going to have the most fun we've ever had in our lives." This too was something Lizzie had read in the brochure. "Park World's the most brilliant place there is," she concluded.

Mrs Moscos, of course, was not convinced. She picked up a blue-grey fern and put it firmly in the hole she'd just dug.

"You only say that because you have never been to the Grand Canyon or to the galaxy of Shawanan, Lizzie Wesson. If you had, you would know how wrong you are. Compared to them, Park World is about as brilliant as a cowpat."

Lizzie was only half listening. She could hear her father shouting to her mother and her sister, Allie, that they had better get a move on or they'd never get to Park World before dark. "Um…" she said.

"Did I not tell you that you have too much luggage?" demanded Mrs Moscos. "You have packed more than the colonists of America, and they weren't planning to return."

"I've got to go now, Mrs Moscos." Lizzie grabbed hold of the bright green straps again and pulled them across her shoulder with a grunt. "I'll bring you back a souvenir."

Mrs Moscos pointed her trowel in Lizzie's direction. "If you really want to have fun and adventure, you must be bold and brave,

Lizzie Wesson. You must take advantage of every opportunity."

"I will," promised Lizzie.

"I don't mean just to play ping-pong," added Mrs Moscos.

But Lizzie was already at the car and didn't hear her.

Lizzie Asks Herself How Much Less Fun She and Charley Would Be Having on the Galaxy of Shawanan

....

The Boogie-on-Down room of the Park World Leisure Complex was crowded, as usual. The nightly disco was one of Park World's most popular attractions. The room throbbed from the music blaring through several speakers, and dozens of smiling people danced beneath the flashing coloured lights.

Lizzie and Charley sat at a table at the edge of the dance floor, but neither of them was smiling. From where they sat, the girls could watch the dancers, but, after three nights of sitting at a table at the edge of the dance floor watching the dancers, this was not a particularly exciting activity.

Charley pushed her crisps away from her with a sound that wavered between a moan and a sigh. "I'm so bored I don't even feel like eating any more," she grumbled.

There were two reasons why the disco was so boring. The first was that everyone else was older than Charley and Lizzie, which meant that they were totally ignored. The only person who'd spoken to them in the three nights they'd been here was the woman who sold the drinks and snacks. The second reason was Lizzie's sister, Allie, and Allie's best friend, Gemma. When Charley and Lizzie got up to dance on Friday night, Gemma and Allie had laughed so hard that the younger girls were forced to sit down again immediately. They hadn't tried dancing since.

Lizzie was twisting her soda straw into knots and wondering if the galaxy of Shawanan could possibly be any less fun than this, but now she looked over at Charley. "You're not more bored than I am," she said. "I've never been more bored in my life."

This was possibly true. Nor was it just the disco that was boring. Park World itself had turned out to be less fun than even Mrs Moscos might have predicted. Indeed, the only thing they'd done that was any fun at all was having silly photographs of themselves taken in the amusement arcade as souvenirs. She and Charley had giggled so much they'd fallen out of the booth.

Lizzie sighed. It really wasn't fair. She'd been so excited about this weekend, and now she would just as soon be home.

Charley would just as soon be home too. She leaned back in her chair, looking grumpy. "I know we're best friends and all, but next time your parents want to take you somewhere, don't ask me to come along." She folded her arms across her chest, which made her look even grumpier. "Because

I won't come. Not even if you're going to Disneyland."

Lizzie's eyebrows came together in a scowl. "What are you saying, Charley Desoto?" she demanded. "Are you saying it's *my* fault we're having such a lousy time?" Lizzie was so shocked by the unfairness of this that she threw the mangled straw across the table at her very best friend in the world. "Are you blaming *me*?" It wouldn't be the first time.

Charley ducked and the straw flew over her head. "Of course I'm not blaming you," she said quickly. Charley's eyes moved towards the dance floor. "We both know whose fault it is we're having such a rotten time."

Lizzie looked towards the dance floor too. The two people to blame for the incredibly bad time Lizzie and Charley were having at Park World were dancing in the middle of the room, waving their arms about and laughing hysterically.

These two people were Allie and Gemma,

of course. Because of several unfortunate past incidents, Mrs Wesson insisted that the older girls keep an eye on the younger ones while they were at Park World. This was a situation that pleased no one. Lizzie argued that she and Charley had been young and irresponsible when these unfortunate past incidents had occurred, but Mrs Wesson wasn't convinced. She said she'd made up her mind, and told them to make the best of it. Allie and Gemma's way of making the best of it was to dedicate themselves to making sure that Lizzie and Charley had the worst time possible. Starting with the disco on Friday night, they had ruined every moment of the weekend that they could.

"I hope they fall over and break their ankles," muttered Lizzie with a good deal of feeling.

"Me too," said Charley. "But even more I hope they lose their voices."

This was a sentiment shared by Lizzie. Unless, as now, Allie and Gemma were too busy having a good time to pay any attention to Lizzie and Charley, they were always shouting at them, making fun of them and bossing them around. The rest of the time, they talked non-stop about themselves.

Lizzie didn't often look on the bright side of things, but now she tried. "At least there's only one more day," she said. "At least there's that."

"One more day…" repeated Charley. "One more day in hell."

Hell was a fairly accurate description of the weekend so far. Allie and Gemma made it very clear on Saturday morning, when they vetoed the water slides in favour of horse-riding, that they were not prepared to do anything they didn't want to do. What they wanted to do was anything that got them near the boys they'd met at the disco on Friday night. The boys were into horses. The riding did not go well. Lizzie's horse suddenly decided to lie down in the middle of the trail, and Lizzie refused to get back on.

"At least neither of us has been seriously injured," offered Lizzie, who was still looking on the bright side.

"No thanks to Allie and Gemma," said Charley sourly.

After the horse-riding, Allie and Gemma wanted to play tennis because the boys were playing on the next court. Neither Charley nor Lizzie had ever played tennis before. As things turned out, this wasn't really a problem, since the only time Allie and Gemma let the ball near either of them was when it accidentally hit Charley on the head. Today Allie and Gemma had insisted on going skateboarding. Neither Lizzie nor Charley knew how to skateboard, but nor did Allie and Gemma. They just wanted to watch the boys. Watching the boys skateboard was boring, but it wasn't as boring as watching Allie and Gemma flirt with the boys. Both Lizzie and Charley fell asleep. Lizzie's nose got sunburned and Charley's foot got cramp.

"Maybe you should talk to your mother," suggested Charley. "I mean, it would be nice if we could do something *we'd* like to do on our last day, wouldn't it?"

"I *did* talk to my mother, remember?" Lizzie kicked the table leg with her foot. "And, anyway, what's the difference? Even when we do something we like they spoil it for us."

This was all too true. This afternoon they'd finally gone swimming, but Allie and Gemma made so much fun of the way they swam, dived and looked in their swimsuits that Lizzie and Charley soon gave up and sat on the side.

"Well, talk to her again," persisted Charley. "Make her understand."

"Make who understand what?"

Lizzie and Charley had been so busy talking that they hadn't seen Allie and Gemma arrive back at the table.

"Nothing," answered Lizzie.

Allie and Gemma flung themselves in their seats. "Here," said Allie, pushing some money towards Lizzie. "Get me and Gemma something to drink."

Lizzie pushed it back. "Get it yourself."

"We're tired," moaned Allie. "We've been dancing for hours. You two've been sitting here doing nothing."

Lizzie turned to Charley in mock horror. "Do you hear that, Charley? Poor Allie and Gemma are exhausted from having so much fun. Doesn't it break your heart?"

"Suit yourself," snapped Allie. "It just so happens that Gemma and I were going to take you two dweebles to the safari park tomorrow, but now I don't think we'll bother."

"Personally, I'd rather play tennis anyway," chimed in Gemma. "Or we could always go riding again," she added sweetly.

Charley and Lizzie exchanged a defeated look.

"OK." Lizzie held out her hand for the money. "But we're going to spend the whole day there?"

"Of course." Allie smiled. "Whatever you want. After all, it is our last day, isn't it?"

Lizzie Makes a Decision out of Boredom, and Charley Agrees out of Hunger

....

The first thing Charley said when she and Lizzie woke up this morning was, "I don't believe it! Even the weather's against us."

She was referring to the rain. After three days of solid sunshine, it was pouring down.

"I don't care if it's snowing," said Lizzie. "They promised to take us to the safari park, and that's where we're going."

Now, sitting at a corner table in the snack bar of the safari park, Charley said, "I don't believe it!" again.

This time Charley was referring to Allie and Gemma.

"I don't believe it." Charley agitated the ice

in her drink with her straw. "They're ruining our last day, just like they ruined all the others."

Lizzie didn't look; she knew what she would see. Allie and Gemma and two boys in baseball caps were shrieking with laughter at a table as far away as they could get from Charley and Lizzie and still be in the same room.

"We should've known they didn't say they'd take us to the safari park because we wanted to go," grumbled Lizzie.

The reason Gemma and Allie offered to take them to the safari park was because they'd made a date with the two boys from the disco. Today was to be devoted to flirting, not to making sure that Lizzie and Charley finally had a good time. Which was why they'd spent most of the morning in the snack bar. There were plenty of things to do at the safari park when it rained, but most of them involved getting at least a little wet. The fact that Park World had actually provided them with bright yellow hooded anoraks made no difference. Allie and Gemma apparently wouldn't be caught dead in bright yellow hooded anoraks. And they definitely weren't about to ruin their hair or their make-up so Lizzie and Charley could see a couple of lions huddled under a tree. In fact, they had no intention of leaving the snack bar at all until the Sea World show in the indoor pool after lunch.

"Didn't I say we should spit in their sodas last night?" asked Charley. "It would've served them right."

"It wouldn't've worked," said Lizzie glumly. "Allie's got the eyesight of Superman."

"Yeah," mumbled Charley, "and the character of Godzilla."

Lizzie's unhappy sigh would have broken even Godzilla's heart. "It's just not fair. There are billions of people in the world. Why do I have to be related to *her*?"

"Shhh!" Charley was looking over Lizzie's shoulder. "They're coming this way."

Lizzie looked round as Allie and Gemma, the boys shuffling behind them, reached the table.

"We're going to play some games until lunchtime," Allie informed them. She nodded towards the bright lights of the arcade. "We'll be in there."

It was clear from her tone that Allie planned to be "in there" without Lizzie and Charley.

"And what are *we* meant to do until lunch?" demanded Lizzie. She was trying hard not to shout, but it wasn't really working. "Just sit here?"

"Well, there's no change there then, is there?" asked Gemma. "That's all you ever do is just sit. The two of you are like statues."

"Or gargoyles," put in Allie.

That remark made even the boys laugh.

"Ha ha ha," Charley muttered under her breath.

Lizzie, however, was screaming in earnest now. "That's not fair!" She banged her fist on the table. "It's *your* fault we haven't done anything all weekend, and you know it!"

For once, Allie didn't scream back. "And you know that that's not true," she answered. Her voice was as sweet as soda. "Gemma and I have taken you everywhere with us. You could've done everything we've done." She squeezed her lips together as though she was going to spit. "If you'd wanted to," she added.

One of the boys cleared his throat. "Maybe they could come to the arcade with us," he suggested.

Both Lizzie and Charley thought this sounded like a pretty good idea, but, before they could scramble to their feet, Allie said, "Oh no, I'm afraid they can't." She shook her head very slowly and sadly. "You see, my little sister just *hates* stupid arcade games." She gave her little sister a sympathetic smile. "Don't you, Lizzie? Isn't that what you said?"

Unfortunately, this was what Lizzie said the last time she and Allie were at an arcade.

It wasn't, however, the whole truth. The remark about hating stupid arcade games was made after an hour and a half of watching Allie play without getting even one go.

"It's not totally true—" began Lizzie, but it was too late to explain. Allie, Gemma and the boys were already walking away.

Charley's stomach rumbled. Although time was moving as slowly as a snail, breakfast still seemed a very long time ago. "Why don't we get something to eat?" she suggested. "That'd be something to do till lunch."

Lizzie scowled. "We didn't come here to eat, Charley. We came to have fun."

Charley scowled back. "The only way we could've had any fun this weekend was if your parents had left Allie and Gemma at home." She stood up. "Come on. I really fancy some chips."

Resigned to the unfairness of her life, Lizzie stood up too. It was then that she noticed a leaflet of the day's events that someone had left on her chair. She didn't remember seeing it when she sat down, but it must have been there because it was wrinkled.

"Maybe I'll get some chocolate too," said Charley. "You know, for the energy." She picked up her bag. "What are you going to have?"

"Number six looks like it might be fun," answered Lizzie.

Charley looked round. Lizzie's eyes were on the leaflet.

"See?" Lizzie pointed to the paper in her hand. *"Number six. Discover the adventure and excitement of the past. Take a ride around beautiful Lake Park World on an eighteenth-century sailing ship."* She looked up at Charley. "Maybe we should do that." She checked her watch. "It starts in ten minutes. If we hurry we can make it."

Charley looked less than delighted. "Are you mad? What about the Gruesome Twosome?"

"What about them?" Lizzie glanced

towards the light and noise of the arcade. Allie and Gemma were hanging on the boys' shoulders, playing some sort of game that required a lot of shrieking and giggling. They wouldn't notice if a troop of aliens marched into the snack bar. "It says here that the ride only takes forty-five minutes," Lizzie continued. "We'll be back before they even know that we're gone."

Charley, however, was in one of her stubborn moods. "What about your mother? She said we must stay with Allie and Gemma."

Lizzie was too fed up by now to pay any attention to what her mother said. "My mother isn't here," she reminded Charley. "So she isn't going to know we disobeyed her, is she?"

"Well…" murmured Charley.

"Come on," urged Lizzie. "This is our last chance to have any fun. It's now or never, Charley. If we don't act now the whole weekend will have been one gigantic waste of time."

But Lizzie had talked Charley into enough things that had turned out badly for Charley to remain cautious. "What about the rain? No one's going to sail around the lake in the rain."

"Of course they are." Lizzie held the leaflet up for Charley to see. "It says right here: *rain or shine.*"

Charley stared at activity number six. Next to the time someone had written the words *rain or shine* in purple ink. She made one last valiant attempt to stay on land. "Since when have you been so keen on boats? I thought you said you'd never get in a boat again after that time in the park."

"I meant rowing boats," said Lizzie, who had meant no such thing. "This is a sailing ship. That's totally different."

Charley, however, was much too stubborn to give in without a struggle. "But the lake's so far away," she argued. "Can't we do something round here?"

Although she couldn't explain why, Lizzie

didn't want to do anything else. Going on the sailing ship suddenly seemed important.

"Please, Charley," she pleaded. "Let's just go and see what it's like. If it looks really awful we don't have to get on. We can just turn round and come back, and by then it'll almost be time for lunch."

It was the mention of lunch that finally won the argument. Charley knew that it would feel like hours until lunch if they stayed in the snack bar, but if they walked down to the lake it would feel more like minutes.

"All right." She gave in. "But we're just going to look, right?"

Lizzie swung her bag over her shoulder. "Right. We're just going to look."

Ship Ahoy!

Lizzie and Charley stood side by side outside the snack bar, watching the rain fall over the rolling green hills and the path that led to the lake.

"I don't see anyone who looks like they're going to the sailing ship," Charley commented after several seconds. "Maybe the ride has been cancelled."

"It hasn't been cancelled," said Lizzie confidently. Lizzie never sounded more confident than when she didn't really know what she was talking about. "The leaflet said *rain or shine*, remember?"

"Well, you'd think there'd be *somebody* else going to the lake," insisted Charley.

"They're probably already down there." Lizzie pulled up the hood of her anorak and prepared to step into the downpour. "I bet it's one of Park World's biggest attractions. Everybody will want to get to it early. We'd better hurry or the ship will be gone before we get to the dock."

The lake proved to be further than they'd thought.

"If I'd known how far it was, I'd've got those chips after all," Charley panted as they struggled through the rain. "You know how hungry running always makes me."

"Everything makes *you* hungry," grunted Lizzie. She came to a stop as the fairy lights and coloured flags of the dock finally came into view.

Charley came up beside her, squinting through the rain. Her eyes moved from one end of the lake to the other. "I don't see any old sailing ship," she announced. She glanced over at Lizzie. "Didn't I say they'd cancel it because of the weather?"

Lizzie sighed very loudly. Charley was always saying "I told you so". It was one of her most annoying habits. The fact that

Charley was often right didn't make Lizzie feel any better about it.

It certainly wasn't making her feel any better now. From where they were standing, Lizzie could see trees, and ducks, and benches, rowing boats, paddle boats, a canoe, and even a floating platform. But she didn't see anything that looked like an ancient sailing ship.

Lizzie, although she would never admit it, could be just as stubborn as Charley. She glanced at her watch. The ship wasn't due to leave for another five minutes. "It has to be there," she decided. "We just can't see it because of the rain."

"We can see everything else," said Charley. "The rowing boats … the paddle boats … the canoe—"

"What's that?" Lizzie grabbed Charley with one hand and pointed with the other. "Over there, in that cove."

Charley's eyes moved along the shore again until she found the tiny cove, huddled by trees. Although she had seen nothing there a few seconds before, there was definitely something bobbing on the water now. "You mean that blue and red thing?" she asked unenthusiastically.

"It's not a *thing* – it's a sailing ship," said Lizzie with great assurance. "Can't you see the sails?"

Charley peered through the rain. The red and blue thing was little more than a blur, but she could see that the red was actually luminous triangles that could be described as sails.

This might have been a good time for Charley to mention that the cove was empty the last time she looked, but – possibly unfortunately – she didn't. Instead she said, "What's it doing over there, then? Shouldn't it be at the dock? I thought boats left from the dock."

Despite the fact that her entire nautical experience was limited to fifteen minutes in a rowing boat, Lizzie shook her head very firmly. "Not sailing ships," she informed Charley. "Sailing ships are different." Lizzie started walking again. "Come on. There's a path over there that looks like it leads to the cove. Let's see if the ship is going on a trip."

"I don't know about this." Charley stood still, as though rooted to the ground. "It doesn't look like an ancient sailing vessel to me. Maybe we should just go back to the snack bar."

"After coming all this way? And what do we do then? Just sit around some more?"

As much as she disliked the look of those luminous red sails, Charley disliked the idea of sitting in the snack bar even more. "Well…"

Lizzie heard the hesitation in her voice. "Come on!" She grabbed Charley's hand. "It'll be leaving soon. Let's take a look since we've come all this way."

Because they were a bit irritated with each other, neither Lizzie nor Charley said anything as they made their way to the lake.

It was Charley who finally broke the silence.

"Good grief!" she cried, coming to an abrupt halt at the water's edge. "What on earth is that?"

"It's the sailing ship." Lizzie said this with her usual confidence, very much as though the sight of the boat hadn't surprised her too.

"It doesn't look like any boat I've ever seen," said Charley.

The truth was that it didn't look like *anything* either of them had ever seen, unless it was an upside-down bucket – a large, glowing, upside-down blue bucket hung with so many sails it looked as if it were surrounded by a shining red cloud.

Lizzie, however, wasn't about to admit this either. "It's because it's been specially made for Lake Park World," she explained. "You know, like the special Park World bus." The special Park World bus resembled a very large golf cart more than an everyday bus.

Charley frowned. "But it's so small."

Which was true. Though large for a bucket, it was very small for a sailing ship.

"Well, it's a small lake," countered Lizzie.

"But it doesn't even have a steering wheel."

Lizzie bit her lip in annoyance. Charley was right again. Not only was the sailing ship shaped rather like a bucket, which was unusual enough, but it was also notable for the fact that it didn't have a helm of any description.

"It must have a steering wheel – somewhere," insisted Lizzie. "And it does have sails."

Indeed the boat had twenty-four sails, which, considering its size, was at least eighteen too many.

"It doesn't look right to me, Lizzie." Charley shivered even though the day, though wet, was far from cold. "That's not an eighteenth-century sailing ship. It's made of metal. Eighteenth-century sailing ships were made of wood."

"Um duh…" Lizzie rolled her eyes as though this was one of the dumbest things she'd ever heard. "It's only a replica, Charley, remember? It's not a real antique."

"But what's it a replica of?" demanded Charley. "The sails are the wrong size, and the wrong colour, and they all go in the wrong direction."

Charley was right again. The ship had one very large sail sloping across one end, and twenty-three very small ones strung across the other end rather like washing on a line.

"I told you," snapped Lizzie. "It's a special Park World sailing ship, isn't it?"

"Well, if it's a special Park World sailing ship, where is everybody? We haven't seen another single person since we left the snack bar."

"That's because they're all already on the ship, isn't it?"

"Well..." Charley sighed. She was too wet and tired to argue any more. "I suppose so." Her stomach reminded her it was there. "We'd better go back," she said. "It must be almost lunchtime."

Lizzie glanced at her watch. They must have walked a lot faster than she'd thought, because barely a minute had passed since she last checked the time.

"We've got ages till lunch. Why don't we wait on the boat till it stops raining?"

Charley was looking at her own watch now, frowning in a puzzled way. "That's funny. It has to be later than that. I'm sure—"

"I bet there'll be something to eat on board," coaxed Lizzie. "You know, sandwiches – and a nice cup of tea."

The words "sandwiches" and "tea" had the desired effect. They put all thoughts of time out of Charley's mind.

"Go on then," said Charley. "Lead the way."

Lizzie and Charley Find More on the Sailing Ship than Sandwiches and Tea

....

Closely followed by Charley, Lizzie crossed
the narrow gangplank and climbed aboard
the tiny boat. As soon as her feet touched
the deck, she stood still and looked around.
Lizzie was very certain that she had never
seen anything like the Park World sailing ship
before, and yet she was suddenly overcome
with a sense of familiarity. It wasn't that she
felt she had been here on this boat before;
it was more that she felt she had been
somewhere very similar. But that, of course,
was completely ridiculous. Lizzie lived on
Meteor Drive and rarely went further than
the shopping centre or the cinema. There was
nothing in either of those places that was

even vaguely like this. And yet there was definitely something that this moment reminded her of. She couldn't shake off the feeling that something unexpected was about to happen – something she should be expecting. Deciding that this feeling must be a memory from a dream, Lizzie pushed it away. Which, as things turned out, was probably not the best thing to do.

"Hello?" called Lizzie in a loud, bright voice. "Hello?"

The only sounds that came back were the pounding of her heart and the falling of the rain.

She took a deep breath and called a little more loudly and more brightly, "Hello? Hello? Is anybody there?"

Charley tugged on her arm. The ship was obviously making her nervous too. "There's no one here, Lizzie. We'd better go."

Lizzie shook off Charley's hand. "Everybody must be inside," she decided. "Come on."

There were four steps in the middle of the

deck that led down to a metal door. Ducking under the fluttering sails, Lizzie walked to them and slowly descended. Charley scuttled after her.

"Hello?" Lizzie raised her fist and knocked firmly but politely on the door. "Hello? Is anybody there?"

Charley gave Lizzie's arm another tug. "I told you so," she hissed. "There's no one here. Let's go."

If Charley hadn't said "I told you so", Lizzie might have given up at that point. But Charley had said "I told you so", just as she always did, and so Lizzie took a deep breath and reached out for the shining silver handle on the door.

"Be careful," warned Charley. "You don't know what's inside."

"That's why I'm opening it, isn't it?" Lizzie whispered back. "So I can find out." But she closed her eyes as she pulled on the handle.

Because Charley's eyes were still open,

it was she who gasped as though she couldn't believe what she saw behind the door.

"Good grief!" gasped Charley. "Lizzie! Look at that!"

As exclamations of surprise go, Charley's "Good grief!" held more pleasure than terror.

Lizzie opened her eyes.

Lizzie hadn't precisely expected to find a Park World guide and a party of Park World guests with their cameras and camcorders behind the door, but she'd certainly hoped she would. Unfortunately, there weren't. Instead, behind the small door was a very large room filled with so many plants and trees it might have been outdoors. No wonder Charley sounded as if she couldn't believe what she saw. Lizzie couldn't believe it either.

"Wow!" breathed Lizzie. "It's as big as the Boogie-on-Down room at the hotel."

In fact, the room behind the door was much larger than the Boogie-on-Down room at the hotel. Which was rather puzzling, since the strange little boat didn't look as if it could hold more than four people, none of them very big, and this room could easily hold four hundred if the trees and plants were removed.

Lizzie continued to stare unblinkingly at the room, wondering how something so large could possibly fit into something so small – and why an ancient sailing ship should be filled with trees and plants.

Charley, however, was distracted from thinking about questions of size and colour. She gave Lizzie a poke. "Not that. I meant look at the table."

Lizzie's eyes searched through the vegetation until they found the small table and two chairs tucked into a wall of pink and purple ferns in the furthest corner. On the table were a tempting plate of sandwiches and a steaming pot of tea.

Relief at seeing something so normal made Lizzie's voice quite loud. "See, what did I tell you?" she crowed. "Didn't I say there'd be food?"

Speed was not normally Charley's most outstanding quality, but on this occasion she reached the table first, threw herself into the nearest chair and pulled the plate of sandwiches closer. "This is more like it," she declared.

But Lizzie's relief at the sight of the food was short-lived. She was not a particularly curious girl, but she couldn't help wondering why there was nothing in the room but plants and a table and two dining chairs. There weren't even any windows, just three small portholes, all in a row, and all partially hidden by a giant palm tree. What was the point of a scenic cruise round Lake Park World if no one could see the scenery? And where were the chairs for everyone else? More importantly, where were the people to sit in the chairs and eat the sandwiches and look out of the windows that weren't there either?

Once again, Lizzie had the feeling that she had experienced something very similar to this before. In fact, the feeling was even stronger now. So strong that she could see herself standing in a Happy Burger restaurant with Charley. There were food and drinks on the tables, but no one else in sight. Lizzie didn't know where this image came from, but as impossible as it seemed she was uneasily certain that it was a memory and not a dream.

"I wonder where everybody else is," mused Lizzie. "Charley, don't you think it's weird that there's nobody here?"

Apparently, Charley didn't think it was weird at all.

"Wow, look at this!" called Charley. "Cheese ... tuna ... even curried chicken salad. Curried chicken salad's my favourite."

"And there isn't any sign of anyone either..." Lizzie continued. "No jackets, no umbrellas ... not even any wet footprints."

"Um..." Charley bit into a sandwich.

"The curried chicken is out of this world."

Lizzie finally went over and sat down across from her. "Don't you think it's strange, Charley? There's all this food and there's no one here but us…"

But the curried chicken was making it difficult for Charley to worry, let alone think. "I'm sure there's some logical explanation," she mumbled. "Why don't you pour the tea? A cup of tea will make you feel better."

Lizzie very much wanted to feel better. And the smell of the tea was so normal and so comforting that she did as Charley asked and poured two large cups of tea. The tea was delicious. Lizzie helped herself to a sandwich. That was delicious too. The room was warm and dry, and cosy because of all the plants. Lizzie began to relax.

She leaned back in her chair, chewing contentedly. "Admit it, Charley. This is much better than that boring old snack bar, isn't it?"

"Way better," Charley admitted. This time she helped herself to a cheese sandwich with cucumber and tomato. "And the food's better too."

"And it's not so noisy," added Lizzie.

"And we don't have to watch Allie and Gemma having a good time," offered Charley. She picked up her cup and raised it to her mouth as the boat gave a sudden lurch. Tea spilled over the top of the table.

Lizzie put down her sandwich. "What was that? Are we moving?"

"Of course we're not moving." Charley wiped the tea from her hand with a serviette that had also been thoughtfully provided. "We're just rocking a bit. We are on water, you know."

Lizzie, however, was now staring at the porthole behind Charley's head with a look on her face that might have been either astonishment or simple terror.

"No we're not." She said this very softly.

Charley sipped her tea. "What do you

mean we're not on water? Of course we're on water. We're on a boat."

Lizzie nodded very slowly. "But we're not on water, Charley. Not as we know it."

It was now Charley's turn to experience the feeling that a moment very much like this moment had happened before. Her heart started to race, but Charley herself was as still as a dead sea.

"Lizzie…" Charley's voice was as flat as a dead sea too. "Lizzie, what are you talking about?"

Lizzie's eyes were still focused on what she could see of the porthole. "Clouds. I can see clouds."

Charley swallowed hard. "What kind of clouds?"

Trying to stay calm, Lizzie took a deep breath. I'm not going to get upset, she told herself. Charley was right before when she said that there had to be a logical explanation. There had to be a logical explanation for this too. If only Lizzie could work out what it was.

"The kind that are in the sky," she replied.

Very, very slowly, Charley turned to face the porthole behind her. "Oh no!" she moaned. "It *is* clouds." She turned back to Lizzie. "Didn't I say we should go back to the snack bar?" Her voice wobbled. "Now what are we going to do?"

"There's no need to panic," said Lizzie, as much for her own benefit as for Charley's. "This is Park World, remember?" And then she laughed with relief as the logical explanation she'd been looking for suddenly occurred to her. That was it, of course! How could she be so silly? This wasn't the real world. This was Park World. It was a place full of fun and adventure for the whole family. A place where the extraordinary was commonplace. "We're not really floating in the sky. This is just one of the exciting attractions."

Charley still had an expression on her face that suggested a great deal of panic, but she was willing to be convinced. "Really?" She glanced back at the porthole as several more clouds drifted by. "Are you sure? I've never heard of an exciting attraction that involves a flying boat."

"But that's the point, isn't it?" Lizzie gave another laugh of relief. "It's not *really* flying, Charley. It's just an illusion."

Charley watched as they broke through the rain clouds and came into a patch of blue. "Well, it's a very convincing one. Now we're above the rain."

"Charley, be reasonable," pleaded Lizzie, who was trying very hard to be reasonable herself. "It has to be a ride. And we're moving, right? Well, if it's moving, then there has to be someone at the controls."

"Well…"

"So all we have to do is find the person who's driving."

"And how are we meant to do that? I'm not going out on that deck again."

Lizzie looked around, as though she might

have missed a list of instructions taped to the wall. There was the door they came in through. There were the three portholes. And there, only a few metres away from them, was a trapdoor embedded in the floor. Lizzie was so excited she leaped to her feet.

"There, Charley. There's another door. Whoever's driving must be down there."

Charley did not leap to her feet. "That door wasn't there before."

Lizzie could only hope that this wasn't true. "Of course it was. You just didn't see it because you were more interested in lunch."

As certain as Charley was that the door had only just appeared, she knew that there was a possibility that she hadn't seen it because her attention was on the sandwiches and tea. With a great show of reluctance, she finally stood up.

"Never again," Charley muttered as she shuffled across the room behind Lizzie. "Do you hear me, Lizzie Wesson? This is definitely the last time. I'm never going to let you talk me into anything ever again."

Lizzie wasn't listening. "Oh no..." she groaned. "There's no handle."

"Because every time I let you talk me into something, things go wrong." Although Charley wasn't really sure what she was talking about, she was starting to remember some incidents she had entirely forgotten until now. "Remember the Happy Burger? Remember the cinema? Remember—"

Lizzie too was starting to remember. But what she remembered was a door in a place she couldn't possibly have been before that flew open at a touch.

Afraid to be wrong, and afraid to be right, Lizzie touched the door in front of her. It flew open.

"Oh my gosh!" gasped Charley.

Falling to their knees, the girls stared into the hole in the floor.

Beneath the trapdoor lay another room even larger than the one they were in. It was walled in glass and banked by control consoles, very much like the sort you might find in a spaceship. Through the wall of glass the girls could see the churning, spangled stars of space. At the main console, which, interestingly enough, featured the large wooden steering wheel of a sailing ship, stood a short figure wearing an old-fashioned naval jacket and a pirate's hat with a very large and very bright blue feather in it.

"Good grief!" cried Charley. "It's Captain Cod!"

Captain Cod was the jolly pirate whose smiling face appeared on the packet of Charley's favourite fish fingers. Captain Cod always wore an old-fashioned naval jacket and a pirate's hat with a large blue feather. Although it wouldn't be particularly surprising to find Captain Cod at Park World since he did make frequent public appearances, Lizzie knew from the way her heart had stopped beating that the figure at the helm was not Captain Cod.

Nonetheless, because she didn't want to give Charley the opportunity to say "I told you so" again, Lizzie turned to her with a hopeful smile. "You see? Captain Cod! Didn't I say we're on a boat?"

The figure at the helm chose that moment to turn round.

Lizzie and Charley opened their mouths to say something – to say, in fact, "Good grief, it's Mrs Moscos!" – but neither of them made a sound. This was the unexpected thing that they should have expected. They both knew that now.

"Do stop gawping like that," ordered Mrs Moscos. "And I will thank you to remember, Lizzie Wesson, that this is a ship, not a boat." She turned round again and grasped the wheel with both hands. "And now if you would be good enough to take your seats, it is about time that we headed for the sea."

Lizzie and Charley Discover that There Are More Seas than They Remember from Their Geography Lessons

....

Although Park World was obviously not the sort of place where they would expect to run into her, neither Lizzie nor Charley was as surprised to see Mrs Moscos as you might suppose. Among the things they were rapidly remembering were other times she had turned up in unlikely places, doing unlikely things.

"I don't see how we can be heading for the sea when we're nowhere near a coast," said Charley as she obediently sat down in one of the two reclining chairs behind the captain's console.

"Nor are we on water," replied Mrs Moscos evenly. "So the question of being near a coast is not particularly relevant, is it?"

"W-w-well, no," stammered Charley. "I don't suppose it is."

Lizzie smiled to herself. She was so used to Mrs Moscos snapping at her that it was very pleasant to have her snapping at Charley for a change.

"So which sea *are* we going to, Mrs Moscos?" asked Lizzie. "The North Sea?" The North Sea was one of the three seas that Lizzie could actually name.

"The North Sea?" Mrs Moscos snorted derisively. "Did I not just say that we're not on water?" The blue feather on her hat bobbed. "We are going to the Lapadala Sea, of course."

Lizzie could see no "of course" about it. The Lapadala Sea was not only not on Lizzie's list of nameable seas, it wasn't a sea she had ever heard of. Lizzie looked over at Charley.

Charley could name two more seas than Lizzie, but it was clear from the expression on her face that the Lapadala was not among them either.

"We've never heard of the Lapadala Sea," Lizzie admitted.

Mrs Moscos glanced at them over her shoulder. Her eyes were narrowed. "And that proves precisely what?" she wanted to know. "Have you ever heard of Breeltop or Sashamonga either?"

Lizzie and Charley shook their heads.

"You see?" Mrs Moscos turned back to steering them round a cluster of stars. "There are far more things in the universe that you two haven't heard of than things that you have heard of."

Lizzie and Charley exchanged another look.

"Well, where is this Lapadala Sea then?" demanded Lizzie.

Mrs Moscos looked round again. "It is not in Park World, that is for certain," she coolly

-66-

informed them. "You will not find a picture of it in your brochure."

"Mrs Moscos, look out!" shrieked Charley. A wave of meteors was racing towards them through the ship's window.

"I am not in another room, Charlene. There is no need to shout." Mrs Moscos jerked the wheel, and the ship rocked as they soared out of the meteors' path.

Charley groaned. This was already proving to be a lot more of an adventure than she had bargained for.

"And no groaning either," ordered Mrs Moscos. "You people are the litterbugs of the universe, so naturally there is a great deal of debris from human space stations around here. I need to concentrate."

"But I don't feel very well," protested Charley. The view of the spinning cosmos surrounding them and the rocking of the ship weren't agreeing with her curried chicken salad sandwich. Indeed, Charley was beginning to feel that she would never eat another curried chicken salad sandwich for as long as she lived. "I got sick on the ferry to France, and that was a lot calmer than this is."

"Fiddlesticks and builders' bricks," said Mrs Moscos. "Pirates don't get seasick. I've never heard of such a thing in my life."

Lizzie was feeling a little queasy herself and had been staring at her feet, but now she looked up. "Pirates? Are you saying we're going to the Lapadala Sea to be pirates?"

"Only of the best sort," Mrs Moscos replied.

But if Mrs Moscos thought the girls were going to take this as good news, she was unhappily mistaken.

"Pirates?" Lizzie and Charley repeated together. "We're going to be pirates?"

"And can you think of a better reason for going to Lapadala?" Mrs Moscos eyed her quizzically. "I certainly can't."

"I can't think of any reason," Lizzie answered truthfully. "I still don't even know where it is."

Fortunately – and for once – Mrs Moscos was actually willing to explain.

The Lapadala Sea, said Mrs Moscos, was on the fifth moon of Umu. It was located deep in a treacherous mountain range, and obscured by a thick covering of red and blue clouds.

"You mean red and blue like this ship?" enquired Charley.

Mrs Moscos gave her a small but approving smile. "Precisely." She spun the wheel, and the ship cut round a speeding piece of metal decorated with a picture of the American flag. "It is not, as I'm sure you can imagine, the sort of place one visits for a holiday, or because one happens to be passing through, you see," explained Mrs Moscos. "One must be quite determined to reach the Lapadala Sea."

Charley didn't like the sound of this at all. "But that's not a reason for going," she muttered. "That's a reason for staying away."

Despite her reluctance to spend even ten

more minutes in the snack bar of the safari park, Lizzie couldn't have agreed more. It didn't seem to her that a trip to a place that sounded as unpleasant as the Lapadala Sea could possibly be necessary.

Although Lizzie knew better than to express this opinion out loud, Mrs Moscos turned again to glare at her.

"Of course it is necessary. Unlike you, Lizzie Wesson, I never do anything that is not necessary. In this case, however, it is more than necessary. It is absolutely vital. Nothing less than the future of the universe depends on it."

"The future of the universe depends on a place no one's ever heard of?" asked Lizzie.

"On a place *you've* never heard of," Mrs Moscos corrected her.

Apparently, the fact that it was so remote and difficult to reach meant that the Lapadala Sea had become an important port for ships crossing the four central galaxies for plunder and illegal trade.

"Nowhere, but between everywhere, the Lapadala Sea is one of those places that attracts criminals and adventurers," said Mrs Moscos. "Much like the Spanish Main." She yanked the wheel sharply and they rose into a cloud of stardust. "At the moment, there is a ship resting on the Lapadala Sea that is carrying a very special cargo – one that cries out to be seized by pirates such as you and I."

Lizzie felt a thrill run down her spine. "You mean treasure?" She rather fancied herself as a treasure hunter.

"Precisely." Mrs Moscos swung them over a spiral of gases. "Indeed, this ship has aboard it one of the greatest treasures in the universe."

As unwell as she still felt, even Charley couldn't help being interested in this information. One of the greatest treasures in the universe was worth a little vomit. "Really? And we're going to get it?"

"What is it?" asked Lizzie with growing excitement. "Gold coins and jewels?"

"No, no, no…" chanted Mrs Moscos. "Not mere stones and metals that are easily replaced. The cargo on this ship is truly valuable. Priceless, in fact."

"What's more valuable than diamonds and gold?" asked Charley.

Seeing the look this question got from Mrs Moscos, Lizzie was very glad she hadn't asked it.

"Life," replied Mrs Moscos simply. "This ship is carrying the last members of several species from different planets in each of the four central galaxies."

Lizzie's father was always watching wildlife documentaries on television. Lizzie found them rather dull compared to pop music videos and soaps, but now she was almost glad he made her watch them with him.

"You mean endangered species, don't you, Mrs Moscos?" Lizzie was quite chuffed that she had the right answer for once. "Like tigers and gorillas and manatees."

Mrs Moscos, however, was not as

impressed by this display of knowledge as Lizzie. "It is similar. But these species are not just endangered. The creatures aboard this ship are the very last of their kind. And all are from planets that have ceased to exist as far as living on them is concerned."

"So what is this ship they're on?" asked Charley. "Is it like the Ark?"

"Not precisely." Mrs Moscos's voice was dark with disapproval. "The purpose of the Ark, as you will recall, was to preserve life – not market it."

One being – she told them – was responsible for most of this destruction. And now, having slaughtered scores of species and made their planets uninhabitable, this ruthless leader was now transporting the surviving creatures to the greatest safari park in the cosmos.

"A safari park?" Lizzie couldn't hide her surprise. "You mean like the one at Park World? Is he going to train them to jump through hoops, and count to twenty, and stuff like that?"

"Jumping through hoops? Counting to twenty?" Mrs Moscos's lips formed a single, displeased line. "And is that meant to be entertaining or to be educational?"

Lizzie didn't answer. She was more or less literally staring into space, frowning in thought. A memory that was so buried that it might never have existed was struggling to get to the top of her mind. It was the memory of a private zoo on a planet far from Earth. One of the exhibits in this zoo was a Happy Burger restaurant filled with people eating Happy Burgers.

"Ah, good." Mrs Moscos sounded unusually pleased. "You are finally remembering and starting to think. And you are right, which always makes a welcome change. It is so much more helpful if you have some idea of what we're doing. This safari park I am speaking of is, indeed, an extension of that very private zoo that you have just remembered, Lizzie. It is to be a tourist attraction and source of amusement for his allies and friends."

"Good grief!" gasped Charley. She turned to Lizzie. "I remember it, Lizzie! I remember being in the zoo!"

"So do I." Lizzie concentrated very hard, trying to dredge up more memories. The name of the planet with the private zoo suddenly popped into her head. "Wei!" cried Lizzie. "It was the planet Wei!" She vividly recalled crossing the silver sands of Wei with Charley and Mrs Moscos. She remembered being chased by a Wei warship. And she, like Charley, suddenly remembered the name of the ruthless ruler of Wei as well.

"You don't mean Louis Wu?" Lizzie and Charley blurted out together.

Mrs Moscos showed neither surprise nor pleasure that they should know this. "And who else would it be?" The blue feather on the pirate's hat bobbed unhappily. "If there is half a penny to be made, Louis Wu will find a way to make it." Mrs Moscos sighed. "As with you humans, there are times when one almost has to admire his cleverness and determination."

Louis Wu had been destroying and looting other planets and even galaxies for millennia, just to make himself more powerful and rich. He had obliterated thousands of species – and for what? For coats, for handbags, for shoes, for jewellery, for fuel, for exotic foods and medicines, for trinkets and doodahs to adorn the wealthy and their homes. Even those most amazing of creatures, the lermins of Mecloa, who could transform themselves into anything they wanted at will, had not been safe from Louis Wu.

It didn't seem logical to Lizzie that anyone would wipe out whole species just to make handbags. "He must've had better reasons than that."

"Not really," said Mrs Moscos. "You know Louis Wu. He can never let anything just be. He'd sell the stars out of the sky if he could."

"Is that why we have so many endangered creatures on Earth?" asked Lizzie. "Because of Louis Wu?"

"Of course not." Mrs Moscos sighed. "You humans have managed that all on your own. By the time Louis Wu got around to your planet there wasn't much left worth plundering."

"I still don't see where we come into this," said Charley.

"Oh don't you?" Mrs Moscos's eyes were on the group of small planets they were passing, but both Lizzie and Charley could tell what expression was on her face, and it was one they were happy enough not to see. "I should think that was obvious. You and I must rescue the creatures on the ship before it returns to Wei. After what happened the last time we three were on Wei, it would be better if we acted while the ship is still on the fifth moon of Umu."

Since she really hadn't enjoyed being in Louis Wu's zoo, this struck Lizzie as a very sensible plan, though not one without problems. "But how exactly are we going to do that, Mrs Moscos?" This was the part that seemed tricky to Lizzie.

"We will go up to the captain of the Wei ship and we will ask him please to hand over his cargo," replied Mrs Moscos.

Charley, possibly because everything, including them, was moving very quickly, failed to hear the sarcasm in Mrs Moscos's voice. "Really? We just have to ask?"

Mrs Moscos risked collision with a bright orange moon to give Charley an unpleasant look. "I am taking into account your weakened condition, Charley, and will assume that your upset stomach has somehow affected your brain. No, we do not just have to ask. We must use the transporter to get them to our ship without the Weis finding out."

Lizzie remembered the transporter she'd used to get the people from the Happy Burger back to Earth, but that didn't answer all of her question. "Where are we going to put them all?" she asked. "This is a very small ship."

Mrs Moscos raised one eyebrow. "Is it?" she enquired. She spread her arms wide. "Is our ship smaller than this room? Is it smaller than the room where Charley ate so much that she made herself ill?"

Lizzie could feel her face go red. The ship, of course, was much smaller than either room.

"Space, like time, can be deceptive," said Mrs Moscos. "You would both do well to remember that."

Sort of Like Greenpeace but More Like Long John Silver

....

Lizzie and Charley were unusually quiet as the sailing ship that was not a sailing ship but a spaceship – manned by a captain who was not a captain but Lizzie Wesson's neighbour Mrs Moscos – ploughed through a sea of stars.

Charley was quiet because she was finding the turbulence of space considerably more upsetting than the turbulence of the English Channel; and also because she was worried about getting back in time for dinner, should she feel like eating by then.

Lizzie was quiet because she was finding speeding through the cosmos considerably more interesting than being yelled at by her sister. When she was on Earth, Lizzie never really noticed the stars or the moon because she was always so busy talking, or watching TV, or thinking about what she wanted to buy. But in space there were so many stars and moons that she couldn't help noticing them. They made her feel oddly calm.

As their ship neared the fifth moon of Umu, Lizzie finally broke the silence.

"This isn't so bad, really, is it?" Lizzie had been giving not just the stars but their mission itself some thought. "It's like being in Greenpeace and rescuing whales," she continued, showing that she had learned more from her father's wildlife documentaries than might have been supposed. Lizzie's father said that the whale rescuers were modern heroes. Which meant that Lizzie and Charley would be heroes too. Lizzie liked the idea of being a hero.

Charley didn't quite see it that way. "I don't feel like a hero," she moaned. "I feel like I'm going to be sick."

"It would be better if you weren't," advised Mrs Moscos. She gestured towards the observation window, where the red and blue clouds of the fifth moon of Umu jammed the sky in much the way that cars had jammed the motorway on the way to Park World. "You are going to have to be very alert down there. Remember, the Lapadala Sea is festering with pirates who are not as good-natured as you and I. You do not want to fall into their claws or paws if you can help it."

Charley was not consoled by this information in the least. "I knew it! We're doomed. We're going to be captured and made to walk the plank."

Choosing to ignore the mention of claws and paws, Lizzie laughed. "Oh, please... We're not going to be captured by pirates. Mrs Moscos is just winding you up. Aren't you, Mrs Moscos?"

Mrs Moscos was concentrating on steering them through a maze of dark mountain passes and didn't look round. "If I were winding you up, you would both be a lot quicker than you are," she answered.

Charley turned her scowling face on Lizzie. "You see? What did I tell you, Lizzie Wesson?" Charley managed to sound very accusing even though she was feeling quite unwell. "Mrs Moscos wasn't kidding. This is what happens when I listen to you—"

Mrs Moscos cut her off. "Fiddledeetosh," she said as the ship at last began to level out. "You have my very solemn word that you are not going to be captured by the pirates of Wei. Now if you will please stop your bickering, we are beginning our descent."

"Really?" Lizzie stood up for a better look.

Above and around them stretched the red and blue clouds of the fifth moon of Umu, but below them lay an enormous open space of rose-tinged gold. Or what would have been an enormous open space if it hadn't been covered with dozens of spacecraft in more sizes, shapes and designs than someone who has always lived on the Earth could possibly have imagined.

Charley stood up too. "Is that the Lapadala Sea, Mrs Moscos?"

"Well, it isn't the swimming pool at Park World." Mrs Moscos pushed some buttons on the console and took her hands from the wheel. "Feast your eyes!" she ordered, gesturing towards the window. "You are the first of your kind ever to see this."

Lizzie peered through the window. Being the first of her kind to see this, she tried to pay more attention than she usually did. Which might explain why she noticed something unusual about the rose-tinged expanse beneath them. Small birds were walking over its surface between the craft, looking for food, very much as though they were walking over the ground. "But it can't be the sea, Mrs Moscos," said Lizzie. "There isn't any water."

Having put their ship on automatic, Mrs Moscos was free to give Lizzie and Charley her full attention. "You are right, Lizzie Wesson. The Lapadala Sea is no longer made of water. Though once, of course, it was." Mrs Moscos shook her head with regret. "It is the same old story, I'm afraid. So many ships have polluted the sea for so many centuries that now it is more like jelly." She sighed philosophically. "Nonetheless, there is always an up side as well as a down, is there not? At least the level of pollution should make you girls feel right at home."

Lizzie, however, had thought of another problem. "But how are we going to find the Weis and sneak on board?" she asked. "There are so many—"

"I, of course, have a plan," interrupted Mrs Moscos. "And I can assure you that there is no sneaking involved in it whatsoever."

Charley looked over at Lizzie.

"No sneaking?" they repeated. "Not even a little?"

"Precisely." Mrs Moscos picked up Lizzie's

bag. "We will walk on board with our heads held high and the captain himself beside us."

"We will?" asked Lizzie.

"We will?" echoed Charley.

Mrs Moscos opened Lizzie's bag and unceremoniously dumped its contents onto a counter. "Of course we will." She put in something that looked like a remote control. Lizzie recognized it at once – it was the transporter they'd used on the planet Wei. "As it happens, the captain of the Wei ship is at this very moment looking for some new crew members with a certain amount of desperation."

Charley and Lizzie exchanged another look. "Crew members?" Their voices lacked enthusiasm. By now they both clearly remembered being chased by Wei soldiers on more than one occasion, which was considerably closer than either of them ever wanted to get again.

"Precisely. That is the crux of my plan, of course. Once on board it will be easy enough to round up the creatures into one place so that they can be transported to the safety of our ship." Mrs Moscos smiled immodestly. "It is a simple plan, but a perfect one, if I do say so myself."

Lizzie wasn't so sure about the perfect part. "But Mrs Moscos, the Weis aren't going to make us members of their crew. We—"

"Are very fortunate," finished Mrs Moscos. "Things are going our way. I have reason to believe that there have been a few distressing incidents with the captive cargo. Which, of course, is not surprising. Weis, as you should know, are better at shooting things than keeping them alive. Unless the creatures are properly cared for, they will not make it back to Wei while they are still breathing. Which would displease Louis Wu very much." She treated them to a sour smile. "I believe we all know how unpleasant Louis Wu can become when he's displeased."

Lizzie could hear Charley swallow hard.

This was obviously something else they both remembered.

"That is why they must find someone who can care for their cargo. The captain and his crew will find themselves in the zoo if they return with nothing but corpses."

It struck Lizzie that there was still a small flaw in Mrs Moscos's plan. "But Mrs Moscos, that doesn't explain why the Weis would hire *us*."

"That's right," chimed in Charley. "Usually they're chasing us."

"Usually is not the same as always," snapped Mrs Moscos. "And to return to your question, Lizzie Wesson, why would they not hire you?" Mrs Moscos closed Lizzie's bag. "It was not my intention to tell them how lazy you both are."

"Thank you," said Lizzie, sounding almost as sarcastic as Mrs Moscos often did, "but that's not what I meant. I meant, won't they be suspicious of us?" It seemed to Lizzie that Mrs Moscos in her Captain Cod gear and she and Charley in their anoraks and hiking boots would stick out like a whale in a school of minnows.

Charley understood. "Because of the way we look," she clarified. "You know – human. And short."

Mrs Moscos gave them one of her less pleasant looks. "Have I ever told you what your problem is?" she enquired coolly. "Aside, that is, from being human?"

"We're lazy?" suggested Charley.

"That too. But also it is that you worry too much." She handed Lizzie her bag. "This is what I mean by travelling light. Everything you need is in here, except, of course, for these." She pulled two pairs of sunglasses with neon-pink frames shaped like stars and two shining red noses from her pocket. "The glasses contain a radio and transmitter so that we will be able to communicate," she explained. "And the noses will help you to breathe, both in Lapadala and on the Wei ship."

Lizzie and Charley, however, were girls who cared a great deal about how they looked. They didn't like to stand out too much. They eyed the noses and the sunglasses warily.

"Do you expect us to *wear* those?" asked Lizzie.

"I expect you to put them on right now, that's what I expect," said Mrs Moscos. "And do be certain that you do not take them off, no matter what excellent reason you have for doing so." She gave Lizzie a stern look. "Is that understood, Lizzie Wesson?"

Lizzie said that that was understood.

"Good," said Mrs Moscos. "I am very glad to hear it." She bent down and opened a hatch in the floor that neither Lizzie nor Charley had noticed before. "And now it is time to visit the town."

Lizzie and Charley peered into the hatch. Below them were islands of blue and red clouds, and below that glinted the golden jelly that was the Lapadala Sea.

"But Mrs Moscos," said Charley, "we're still in the sky."

Mrs Moscos adjusted her hat and straightened her jacket. "How observant of you, Charlene. It is no wonder I brought you along. Obviously we would be totally lost without you."

"I get it!" Lizzie smiled in triumph. "That's why the ship's blue and red, isn't it? So we can hide in the clouds."

Mrs Moscos sat down at the edge of the hatch, her legs dangling through the hole. "Precisely."

"So what are we going to do?" asked Charley. "How do we get down?"

"I should think that would be obvious even to you," said Mrs Moscos. She gave herself a push and immediately dropped through the clouds. "We jump."

Lizzie and Charley Discover Just Whom Mrs Moscos Means When She Uses the Word "We"

···

"Well, girls," said Mrs Moscos. "Take a good look, because this is it!" She spread her arms to indicate the rose-tinged pool of golden goo and the cluster of buildings huddled on its shore. "Beautiful Lapadala-by-the-sea. Or beautiful Lapadala-by-the-jelly, if you prefer."

Lizzie and Charley were trying to wipe the gold-tinged jelly from their anoraks, but at Mrs Moscos's words they raised their heads and took a good look. "Beautiful" was not the word that sprang to either of their minds as a proper description of the town. "Depressing" came to Lizzie's mind; and "scary" came to Charley's.

Lizzie squinted at the ramshackle buildings, all of them rusted, dented and covered with a fine, iridescent lacework. The buildings didn't look as if they'd been laid out in any order, but simply dropped – probably by someone in a bit of a hurry.

"Mrs Moscos?" Lizzie's voice was very soft. "Are those buildings really old spaceships?"

The blue feather bobbed up and down approvingly. "Precisely. Spaceships, starships, schooners, planet hoppers... Whatever has landed and been unable or unwilling to depart. As you may appreciate, it is unwise to leave a ship unguarded around here for longer than a nanosecond, unless you want to find that it's been turned into a hotel."

"But why are they covered in lace?" asked Lizzie. Lace seemed rather dainty for a place that otherwise looked like a rubbish tip.

"They aren't," replied Mrs Moscos. "Those are the tattmatts of 46Z, otherwise known as the barnacles of the central galaxies." She smiled warmly on the tattmatts. "Pretty, aren't they?"

"Pretty creepy," whispered Charley.

Lizzie gave her a poke, and looked to see if Mrs Moscos had heard Charley, but Mrs Moscos was striding on ahead of them. Since this was clearly not the sort of place where children should be left on their own, they scurried after her, careful not to brush against any wall.

Mrs Moscos turned a corner into the main street of Lapadala, and Charley and Lizzie turned too. The only reason the girls didn't scream out loud was because they were too astonished to utter a sound. The main street was full. Lizzie and Charley, who often shopped at the Victoria Shopping Centre, were used to crowds, but even Christmas Eve at the Victoria Shopping Centre hadn't prepared them for the main street of Lapadala on a busy afternoon.

"Good grief," whispered Charley. "It's like a fancy dress party, except nobody's dressed as Barbie or Mickey, or anything like that."

Lizzie's eyes fell on a group of extremely large lizards sitting outside what once had been a flying saucer. They were playing some sort of game with engine parts.

"What are *those*?" gasped Lizzie.

"Bogwamps from Zaza," replied Mrs Moscos.

"Oh my gosh!" cried Charley, trying not to point. "Those pine trees are armed!"

Indeed, four beings who looked remarkably like pine trees wearing heavy black boots and gloves and carrying guns were walking towards them.

"Don't be silly," scolded Mrs Moscos. "Those aren't pine trees. They are space sailors from Mibya." She nodded to the pine trees as they passed, and they nodded back.

Lizzie was still coming to grips with pine trees carrying automatic weapons when she caught sight of a humanoid with two heads and quite a long tail. "What on Earth is *that*?"

"A Quokan mercenary." Mrs Moscos picked up speed. "And I might remind you, Lizzie Wesson, that you are no longer on the planet Earth."

Lizzie rolled her eyes. "I do know that, Mrs Moscos," she said a trifle waspishly. "It's just an expression."

"But one that is totally meaningless here," countered Mrs Moscos. "Indeed, although I have not done a survey myself, I would imagine that Earth is one of the few planets not represented in Lapadala."

Mrs Moscos was probably right. The citizens of Lapadala came in all shapes, sizes, colours and species, and were dressed in everything from metallic jumpsuits to pine needles, but except for the three of them there was no one who looked as if it might be able to name the capitals of Europe.

"Well, at least we don't stand out," said Charley.

Indeed, so eccentric and diverse were the citizens of Lapadala that Lizzie, Charley and even Mrs Moscos would have had to be wrapped in fairy lights for anyone to glance at them even once.

"You should not be standing anywhere," snapped Mrs Moscos. "You should be hurrying to get to the Wei employment office before the jobs are taken."

And what a terrible shame that would be, thought Lizzie.

Nonetheless, she didn't so much as consider dragging her feet the way she did when her mother took her somewhere she didn't want to go. Not that she had much choice. For, unlike Mrs Wesson, Mrs Moscos was not about to stop and wait for Lizzie, or even slow down. Lizzie knew that if she didn't keep up she would be left alone with the giant lizards and their friends.

Mrs Moscos marched through the twisting streets of Lapadala at a brisk pace, Lizzie and Charley trotting breathlessly behind her, until they reached a large square surrounded by cafés and a crowded market.

"At last!" Mrs Moscos pointed across the square. "The Weis are still there. We are not too late."

"I'm glad *she* thinks that's good news," Charley muttered, her eyes falling on the all too familiar uniform of the Wei army.

The Wei employment office consisted of a stall made out of the wing of an abandoned space shuttle and a sign hanging from it that said in several dozen different languages (none of which were English) what Lizzie and Charley assumed to be "crew wanted".

"Gosh," said Lizzie, "the Weis look almost normal next to everyone else, don't they?"

Mrs Moscos sighed. "Trust you to think that humanoid is normal." She stopped abruptly and cast a cold eye upon them. "And from now on, you will both please keep your mouths shut and do exactly as I tell you."

Lizzie had a question. "Mrs Moscos, even if we don't speak, won't the Weis know that we're from Earth?"

"And how would they know that?" asked Mrs Moscos. "They can't smell you because of all the pollution. And with those bright yellow anoraks and distinctive breathing apparatus they will, of course, assume that you are Boragian ramblers."

Oh, of course, thought Lizzie. Boragian ramblers... Why didn't I think of that?

"Boragian what?" asked Charley.

"Ramblers," repeated Mrs Moscos. "Boragian ramblers. Because they spend all their time wandering about, delighting in the flora and fauna of rainy Boragia, they dress as you are dressed – and their noses, naturally, are permanently red from the cold." She sighed wistfully. "Though I am afraid that the similarity does end there."

Boragian ramblers were gentle, intelligent midgets whose only form of communication was a soothing, almost hypnotic, hum.

"Boragian ramblers are both hard-working and unambitious," explained Mrs Moscos. "Because of this and their peaceful natures, they are one of the few species in the cosmos that can get on with the Weis for any length of time. Indeed, they can get on with almost anyone." She smiled slyly. "And that, of course, is why they are famous throughout the galaxies as species trainers."

"Pardon?" said Charley.

"You mean like animal trainers?" asked Lizzie.

"Precisely." Mrs Moscos's smile became a little smug. "Which is why the Wei captain will be overjoyed to see you two. To the best of my knowledge, there do not happen to be any other Boragian ramblers in Lapadala at the moment. And all you two have to do is look blank, which should be extremely easy for you, and hum very softly at all times."

There was something about this scheme that didn't strike Lizzie as right. "But Mrs Moscos—"

Mrs Moscos, however, feather dancing, was already marching towards the Wei employment office on the other side of the square.

By the time Lizzie and Charley caught up with her, she was already in earnest conversation with the Wei captain.

"Gadzaktarmasolata," Mrs Moscos was saying as they arrived at her side. "Rumblestiltonsticks."

Dressed all in black, scarred and unsmiling, the Wei captain looked even less pleasant than Lizzie and Charley had expected. He frowned at each of them in turn, and then looked back at Mrs Moscos. "Bumpleribbon," he said, indicating Charley. He pointed to Lizzie next. "Maladisturgeon."

"Auditraspberrybalsa," said Mrs Moscos. She put one hand on Lizzie's shoulder and one on Charley's, and squeezed.

Looking impressively blank, Lizzie and Charley started to hum more loudly.

It would be inaccurate to say that the Wei captain smiled, but he did look slightly less fierce. He held up one hand, and

Mrs Moscos put her palm against his. "Zadooksinterspit," he said to Mrs Moscos.

"Zadooksinterspit," repeated Mrs Moscos.

Before Lizzie and Charley realized that this was the Wei way of making a deal, the Wei captain was on his feet. He ripped the help-wanted sign from the stall and stuck it under his arm. "Biddletop," he shouted, and with that he started off in the direction of the gelatinous sea.

Her hands still on their shoulders, Mrs Moscos gave Lizzie and Charley a very firm shove forward.

"Hang on!" hissed Lizzie. "What about you, Mrs Moscos? Aren't you coming with us?"

"Naturally not." Mrs Moscos seemed surprised that they might have thought that she was going with them. She gave them each another shove. "I have far too many other things to do. I must get the supplies for the creatures, you know. It may take some time to find them all a new home. They will need plants, rocks, trees, bodies of water... And food, of course." She gave Charley a look. "Only on Earth are curried chicken salad sandwiches considered nutritious."

Lizzie, however, remembered Mrs Moscos saying "we", as in "when we board the ship". "But you said—"

"That was just a figure of speech," cut in Mrs Moscos. "You know, like 'what on Earth'. You must learn not take everything so literally, Lizzie Wesson. You miss the forest for the tree."

Charley didn't like the sound of this at all. "But can't we do the shopping later?" she pleaded. "After we get the creatures on board?"

Mrs Moscos adjusted her hat at a jauntier angle. "And who do you imagine will drive the ship if I go with you? Who will position it so that you can safely get yourselves and those poor creatures into it?"

"But Mrs Moscos..." Charley's voice shook. "What happens if we don't get off the Wei ship?"

"But you will get off the Wei ship," Mrs Moscos assured her. "Because you will have yourselves and all the creatures together in the chamber beneath the cargo-hold by the time the Weis are ready to leave Lapadala."

Moving all the creatures to another place sounded to Charley like it might take a great deal of time and work. "But wouldn't it be easier if we all just stayed in the cargo-hold?" she asked.

Mrs Moscos sighed in a way that suggested that she suffered a great deal from the stupidity of certain human children. "Yes, Charlene, I am sure it *would* be much easier. Unfortunately, due to the fact that the cargo-hold is specially insulated so that nothing can be beamed in or out of it, it would not be nearly as effective. The chamber beneath it, however, is not so protected." She eyed them sternly. "Am I making myself perfectly clear?"

Both girls nodded.

"Good." Mrs Moscos threw back her shoulders and raised her head, a sign that this conversation was almost over. "Hopefully, you do remember that the transporter is in Lizzie's bag. As soon as you hear the engines start, count to ten, then push the blue button. I will be waiting."

Lizzie, however, was all too aware that even when she tried very hard to do as she was told, it didn't always work. "But what happens if we get taken back to Wei by mistake?"

"Well, that does depend, doesn't it?" Mrs Moscos gave them another push. "If the Weis realize that you are not really Boragian ramblers, but two of the most wanted humans in Wei history, they will naturally have you executed."

"Wanted?" asked Lizzie.

"Most wanted?" asked Charley.

"Well, of course." Mrs Moscos seemed surprised that they didn't know this already. "You and I have twice thwarted Louis Wu, have we not? And that has made you very famous. There are even posters."

"Posters?" Lizzie repeated. "Of *us*?" She didn't dislike the idea of being famous enough to be on a poster. "Can we see one?"

"Lizzie, for heaven's sake!" Displaying no sign of the famous gentle Boragian nature, Charley jabbed Lizzie in the ribs. "Will you forget about the posters?" She appealed to Mrs Moscos. "What if the Weis don't realize who we are?" she asked. "What happens then?"

Mrs Moscos smiled as though she had finally reached the good news part of the story. "Then they will keep you to work in the zoo, of course."

Mrs Moscos Forgets Something

....

It was with hearts that were sinking rather like two small ships that Lizzie and Charley followed the Wei captain out of the market square and back through the town to the gelatinous sea.

Charley squeezed Lizzie's hand as something with three heads sped past them, ringing like an old-fashioned telephone. "This place gives me the creeps," she whispered. "I really wish Mrs Moscos hadn't left us like this."

"And I don't?" hissed Lizzie. There were millions – probably billions – of places Lizzie would like to be without Mrs Moscos, but Lapadala was definitely not one of them. It gave her the creeps too. Lizzie's excitement over being a hero was starting to fade.

"It's just that if something goes wrong—"
Charley stopped, suddenly aware of just how
much could go wrong. She swallowed hard.
"I really do think I'm much too young to be
executed."

Lizzie ducked out of the way of an
extremely large bird-like creature wearing
a baseball cap. "And I'm not?"

Their sunglasses crackled. "Who said that
I left you?" asked the voice of Mrs Moscos.
Though it sounded far away and was bristling
with static, the irritation in it came through
loud and clear. "If you girls would talk less
and pay attention more you would know
that I have everything under control, just as
I always do."

Lizzie was so happy to hear Mrs Moscos
that she wasn't even bothered that Mrs
Moscos was snapping at her as usual. She
glanced round, expecting to see the bobbing
feather on the pirate's hat, but there was
nothing behind her but a robot with pulsating
eyes. "Mrs Moscos, where are you?"

"And where would you expect me to be?" was the sour reply. "In Las Vegas? I am just about to purchase some ferns for the lermins, and then I will return to our ship to anticipate your arrival. Which I trust will be quite soon. Have you come upon the Wei ship yet?"

"I think so." Lizzie squinted through her dark glasses. "We are at the sea."

"And there's the Wei ship!" cut in Charley as she spotted a familiar black and silver shape rising above the smaller ships huddled along the coast like a dark cloud. "I'd recognize it anywhere."

"Then pay attention," ordered Mrs Moscos. "As soon as you are alone with the creatures you must prepare them for the transfer. You may have to calm them down a bit after all their time with the barbaric Weis. And then you have to get them underneath the cargo-hold, as I told you before. I shouldn't think the Weis will leave for several hours, but you will want to act quickly so you are ready when they do."

"Oh my gosh!" breathed Charley. "The door's opening."

Indeed, the door to the Wei ship was opening, silently and slowly, yawning before them like a giant mouth, ready to swallow them whole.

Mrs Moscos's sigh echoed with static. "Of course the door is opening. How would you get inside if it didn't open?"

"I don't think this is such a good idea," Charley mumbled. "Isn't there an alternative plan?"

"Of course there is an alternative plan," replied Mrs Moscos. "And this is it. Now get on that ship. The fate of the universe is in your hands."

Lizzie, like Charley, couldn't help wishing that the fate of the universe was in someone else's hands, but there was obviously no turning back now. She squeezed Charley's hand hard as they walked up the gangway.

"What's happening?" asked Mrs Moscos.

"We're going in," whispered Lizzie as she and Charley stepped over the threshold. The door shut behind them so quickly that they jumped.

"Good grief!" yelped Charley.

Up until now, Lizzie and Charley had only seen Wei ships from the outside. From the outside, Wei ships were large and menacing. Now they could see that they were just as large and menacing inside.

Lizzie's heart started to beat faster. There seemed to be an awful lot of armed soldiers about.

"What's happening?" demanded Mrs Moscos.

The captain had come to a halt in the main foyer, and was calling over a soldier with a patch over one eye and a bandage on his hand. There was quite a lot of gesturing and loud talking. Both the captain and the soldier kept pointing at the girls. Whatever the captain was saying, it seemed to be causing the soldier a certain amount of amusement, in a dark and troubling sort of way.

"I think he's having us arrested," reported Lizzie.

"What utter nonsense," said Mrs Moscos. "I can hear them quite clearly now. The captain is merely telling the soldier that you are the new caretakers of the cargo and that he must show you where the creatures are kept."

"Why is the soldier laughing like that?" asked Charley.

"Ah…" sighed Mrs Moscos. "I believe it may be because the soldier was one of the old caretakers. As I told you, there have been a few injuries."

"No you didn't," corrected Lizzie. "You said there'd been some incidents."

"Incidents … injuries… And I did mention that the Weis had turned their captives into rampaging beasts, did I not? If you paid more attention, you would have known precisely what I meant by incidents."

Lizzie might have continued this argument

if the conversation between the captain and the battered soldier hadn't ended abruptly at that moment.

"Uh-oh…" breathed Charley. "He's looking at us."

Not only was he looking at them, but for the first time since they left the square, the captain spoke to them.

"Sizemagraff," said the captain. He made a shooing motion with his hands. "Sizemagraff," he said again.

"He wants you to go with the soldier," Mrs Moscos translated. "Hum loudly, so he knows you understand."

Humming and looking as blank as a clean sheet of paper, Lizzie and Charley followed the soldier down one of the corridors off the main foyer.

"Pay attention," ordered Mrs Moscos. "Keep on the lookout for a purple door."

"Purple?" Lizzie squinted through her sunglasses. Because of them, she couldn't see colours too clearly, but, of course, there weren't really any colours to see. "Everything's black or silver."

Charley poked her. "What about that door over there? That might be purple."

Lizzie looked. "It's got something on it that looks like a W on top of another W," she reported.

"The Wei symbol for flight," Mrs Moscos informed them. "That, girls, is the control room. It might be wise for you to attempt to remember where it is. Just in case."

Not even Charley dared ask just in case of what.

"But it's like walking through a maze!" Lizzie protested. She wasn't very good at mazes. Someone always had to come and get her out.

"Try," advised Mrs Moscos.

Lizzie did try, but she couldn't see that it was going to do her much good. The problem was twofold.

In the first fold was the fact that every corridor looked exactly like the last: smooth metallic walls, smooth metallic floors and smooth metallic doors. The only difference between them was the number of Weis walking along or milling about.

In the second fold was the additional fact that the lighting in Wei ships was not designed for people wearing sunglasses. As far as Lizzie was concerned, she might have been in a land of shadows.

At last they came to the final corridor, deep in the belly of the ship.

The soldier stopped so suddenly that Lizzie and Charley walked right into him.

"Mandelbrot," said the soldier. A door opened in front of him. It was even darker behind the door. Indeed, it was so dark that they wouldn't have known it was open if it hadn't been for the incredible noise that rushed out to meet them. Angry howls, shrieks, growls and grunts flew out of the hold like rocks. Lizzie couldn't be certain – since she couldn't actually see anything – but it sounded to her as if several of the

captive creatures were hurling themselves
at the walls of their cages while others were
trying to claw their way out.

"What's in there? It sounds like a jungle
on a bad day." Charley peered into the
blackness. "I can't see a thing."

"That is because of the very subdued
lighting," explained Mrs Moscos. "The Weis
thought that the creatures might calm down
if they believed it was night." She cleared her
throat. "But, as you can hear, they made a
serious miscalculation."

"What's wrong with the soldier?" asked
Lizzie. She and Charley both had their hands
over their ears, but his hand was over his
mouth.

"Most likely it is the stench," said Mrs
Moscos. "So you may thank me for providing
you with such efficient gas masks."

"The stench can't be worse than this
noise," muttered Charley. "I'm sure I feel
a migraine coming on."

"Begelsluice," gasped the soldier. He

sounded as if he might be gagging. "Introstationaryunderpinning-warringtonblast."

"He is telling you about the creatures," Mrs Moscos translated. "Reptiles on the left, birds on the right, and mammals and whatever-remains at the end. The food is in the cupboard next to the door, as are the water tap and the hose."

"Mopedsingleton." The soldier had been pointing into the cargo-hold, but now he turned to Lizzie and Charley. He moved a finger to his eye, shaking his head. "Beedlefartapplejuicejumpoverroses."

"It is as I suspected. No one has been to feed the captive creatures since he was injured," Mrs Moscos informed them. "I would say that that is one possible reason why they are making so much noise. Obviously you will have to feed them before you can let them out."

The soldier pointed at the opening in the sleek wall. "Beansprout." Lizzie didn't need

Mrs Moscos to translate that. This was not a statement, it was an order. He wanted them to walk through the door.

"I'm not going," she whispered between clenched teeth. "I can't see what's in there."

"I believe we know what is in there," said Mrs Moscos.

Yeah, right, thought Lizzie, rampaging beasts…

"Do stop being so squeamish." Mrs Moscos's voice crackled. "Just get inside that room. The sooner you begin, the sooner it can be over."

Her eyes on the soldier, who was now urging them in with a rather menacing-looking gun, Charley tightened her grip on Lizzie's hand. "We don't exactly have a choice, do we?"

Lizzie was also watching the gun. "Not so you'd notice." She took a deep breath and, humming loudly, she and Charley reluctantly moved under the pointing weapon of the Wci soldier. Unfortunately, because they were so nervous, and could barely see, they missed the doorway and hit the wall.

A hand fell on their shoulders. "Mippopatamus," said the soldier. "Underlupin."

There was something in the way he said these words – and in the way he held her in place – that told Lizzie that something unfortunate was about to happen.

"Ah," said Mrs Moscos. "He doesn't think you need your glasses." She sighed. "Now that is something I didn't think of."

Lizzie tried to hold onto her glasses, but the soldier was too quick and too strong for her. The last thing she heard before he snatched them from her face was a barrage of static and then, sounding very far away and falling apart, Mrs Moscos saying, "—member cracklecrackle – help you cracklecrackle – the lermin…"

"Lermin?" Lizzie couldn't recall what a lermin was. But it was too late to ask Mrs Moscos. Mrs Moscos, like everything else that Lizzie and Charley knew, was gone.

Lizzie and Charley Have Their Second Experience of Life in a Louis Wu Zoo

....

"Think, Charley, think," Lizzie urged in the darkness. "You had the glasses on at least a second longer than I did. Didn't Mrs Moscos say anything else?"

Lizzie's eyes were starting to adjust to the limited light of the cargo-hold. She could see Charley's head shaking back and forth.

"I heard the same thing you heard, Lizzie. She said something about a lermin helping us." Charley rummaged in the pocket of her anorak, hoping to find an overlooked sweet. Charley always tried to find food in stressful situations, and this was definitely a stressful situation. "But I don't know what a lermin is or how it could possibly help us unless it's got an army with it."

Lizzie didn't know either. The only thing Lizzie was sure of was that the creatures didn't like Weis. As soon as the Wei soldier left them, they became noticeably calmer. There was still a lot of unhappy noise, but the clawing and angry howls had stopped completely.

"I expect that's what Mrs Moscos meant when she said that the Weis turned them into rampaging beasts," said Lizzie. "If a Wei came near us, he'd set them all off again, no matter how kind his heart is. And then we'd never be able to calm them down enough to be transported."

"Then what—" Charley broke off as the cages around them finally fell into focus. "Good grief!" she gasped. "Look at this place! It's more like tins of sardines than a zoo."

"Oh my gosh!" Lizzie's voice was barely a whisper. Of all the shocking things she'd seen recently, this was by far the most shocking.

The last time Charley and Lizzie were trapped in one of the attractions of Louis Wu's zoo, the zoo in question was a very well-run model zoo. Each species had a large enclosed cage in which its natural environment had been meticulously recreated. Which was why Lizzie and Charley had found themselves in a perfect reconstruction of the Happy Burger in their local shopping centre (Exhibit 356009A: Humans from Earth).

The makeshift zoo on the Wei ship, however, could only be considered a model if it were a model of how not to treat other creatures. Lizzie had never wanted a hamster because she thought it was cruel to keep an animal in a cage, no matter how big the cage or how small the animal. This was obviously not something that bothered the Weis, however. It was true that the different groups were divided into three glass rooms, but they were packed in with barely enough space for even the smallest to sit down. Not only had the captives not been fed for some time, but they hadn't been cleaned or given water either.

"No wonder it smells so bad," said Charley. "Even in this light you can tell that the cages are absolutely filthy." Her eyes darted from group to group. The reptiles were on the left; the birds were on the right; and dead ahead were the mammals and whatever-remains.

"It's hard to believe they're endangered, isn't it?" asked Lizzie. "There are so many of them..."

Indeed, there were so many of them. Although there were no more than two of each species, the number of species was much closer to two hundred than two.

Lizzie peered intently through the gloom. She could see eyes, teeth, noses, feathers, paws, scales and hair – but none of it was put together in a way that a ten-year-old girl from Earth would find particularly reassuring.

"Do any of them look sort of familiar to you?" she asked uneasily.

"Well…" Charley stared into the dull kaleidoscope of colours that was the cage of birds. There were some that were as small as bees and shone like the glow-in-the-dark stars she'd stuck over her bed. There were others that were larger than her and Lizzie. "Sort of." Charley had once owned a canary and could therefore be considered something of an expert. "Most of them do seem to have wings…"

Lizzie didn't find this much comfort. "But most of them don't seem to have beaks."

"No…" Charley nodded slowly. "No, a lot of them don't have beaks." Indeed, the bird right in front of her had very thick, dark lips and buck teeth. She decided to ignore the fact that she thought she could see a paw or two. She looked over at Lizzie. "So now what do we do?"

The first word that popped into Lizzie's mind was "run". Unfortunately, one of the drawbacks of being on a spaceship was that there wasn't really anywhere they could run.

"Well," said Lizzie, trying to sound like the hero she'd been only a short time ago and not a girl who would be happy to flee if only she could, "I reckon we'd better feed them. Then we can get them ready for transportation."

Charley groaned. "Do we really have to?" She had just switched her attention from the birds to the reptiles, which had turned out to be the wrong thing to do. The reptiles did look familiar. It was true that the details of size and colour, and the number of feet, heads and tails were shockingly different from what she was used to, but on the whole they did seem very reptilian. "It looks like Jurassic Park in there."

Lizzie's love of reptiles, even small ones with only one tail, was no greater than Charley's. Indeed, she had never fully recovered from the day Robbie Stone brought his chameleon into school and it peed on her desk. Nonetheless, the captive creatures all looked so miserable that Lizzie couldn't help feeling sorry for them – even the ones with long tails and scales. Added to that, of course, was her fear of what Mrs Moscos would be likely to say should they fail in their mission.

"It's not like the pick-'n'-mix in the shopping centre," said Lizzie. "I don't think we get to choose which ones we save."

An extraordinarily long, shocking-pink tongue flicked at the glass next to Charley, making her jump.

"Just as long as we don't have to touch them." Charley shuddered. "Just promise me that."

"We're not going to have to touch anything," Lizzie promised. "See?" She indicated the two small doors at the front of the cages, each connected to a trough. "All we have to do is pour the food into one and the water into the other."

Charley peered down at the food and water compartments through the glass. "I think something's been trying to open them from the inside," she said. "They look blocked."

"They can't be!" Lizzie pulled on one of the handles, but the door had been sealed shut.

"So now what?" asked Charley.

Lizzie glanced over at the birds. Like the reptiles and the mammals and whatever-remains, they were pressing against the glass, watching Charley and Lizzie with both curiosity and hope. "Well, I guess we'll have to take the food to them."

"Pardon?" That stubborn look was back on Charley's face. "You do realize that the reason the creatures haven't been fed is because they attacked the last Wei soldier to go near them?"

"You can't blame them for that," argued Lizzie. "He was pretty unpleasant."

Charley looked from Lizzie to the reptiles. "And you think they're not?"

Lizzie did think that some of them looked very unpleasant, but it wasn't a thought she wanted to dwell on. "You can't judge a book by its cover," she answered. "Anyway, we're not going to stay for tea. We'll just shove the food in, and then while they're busy eating we can fill up their water with the hose. It'll be over in no time."

It was the part about it being over in no time that changed Charley's mind. Despite the desperateness of their situation, she was starting to feel a little peckish. With a little luck, they might still make it back in time for supper. But that, of course, meant getting off the Wei ship as quickly as they could.

"All right," Charley reluctantly agreed. "Where do we start?"

Here was a question. Lizzie's eyes moved from the cage on her left, to the cage on her right and, finally, to the cage at the end of the room. In the first, she could see the flicking pink tongue of a Conovan gas snake. In the second she could see a pair of copper-coloured humanoid hands just visible behind the metallic wings of a limea from Galini. But from this distance all she could see in the cage at the end of the room was eyes.

For all she knew, they might be the eyes of cocker spaniels and deer like Bambi. This struck Lizzie as at least hopeful.

"We'll start with the mammals and whatever-remains," Lizzie decided. They could work their way up to birds with hands. And then, more to reassure herself than reassure Charley, she added, "We just fill the feeders, give them some water, and we're out."

But as Lizzie should have learned by now, it is often easier to say a thing than it is to do it.

Lizzie stepped into the mammals and whatever-remains cage first, Charley clinging to her from behind. Lizzie hardly dared to breathe.

She looked down. A small, silver tabby cat, very much like the cat Lizzie had when she was little, had wrapped itself round her ankles and was purring with contentment. "Oh my gosh! It's a cat. It's an ordinary cat."

If Lizzie had thought about it, she might

have realized that the chances of finding
a tabby cat that looked like her cat, Rocky,
on a Wei spaceship were incredibly small.
Indeed, they didn't exist. The creature
rubbing itself against her was, in fact,
a lermin. Mrs Moscos hadn't told them
everything about lermins that there was
to know. It was true that lermins could
transform themselves into anything they
wanted. If they wanted to hide among rocks,
for example, they became rocks. If they
wanted to hide in a flock of birds, they
became birds. But they didn't only change
into things they could see. They could also
turn themselves into others' memories,
dreams and fears as well.

Charley didn't so much as glance at the
lermin. She was otherwise occupied, trying to
avoid the affectionate licks of something that
might have been a giraffe if it hadn't been
black and silver with a single horn in the
middle of its forehead. "They certainly seem
to like us..." she murmured.

"They really do, don't they?" Lizzie bent down and scratched the lermin under its chin. "Didn't I tell you there was nothing to be afraid of?"

"Lizzie," said Charley.

Lizzie tugged playfully at a velvet ear. "You know, whatever this is, it looks so much like Rocky, it's amazing. Don't you think so?"

"Lizzie," said Charley.

Lizzie rubbed the top of a velvet head. "Maybe they know we're here to save them. Maybe that's why they like us so much."

"Lizzie!" Charley's fingers dug into Lizzie's shoulder. "Stop playing with that, whatever it is, and look!"

Lizzie had heard that tone in Charley Desoto's voice before, especially when they were somewhere other than Earth. She was about to panic. Lizzie looked up.

"Oh," said Lizzie.

Dozens of mammals and whatever-remains were slowly, but very surely, advancing on them from all sides.

"I knew something like this would happen!" Charley wailed. "They're going to eat us. Why should they want dumb old dry food when they can have fresh human flesh?"

Lizzie was determined not to catch Charley's panic. "They're not going to eat us," she said very firmly. She was fairly certain that this was true. Although the creatures were all moving towards them, they were more like dogs that wanted to be petted than savage bears that wanted supper. On the other hand, there was the possibility that they might smother Charley and Lizzie with love. "Back out!" ordered Lizzie. "Just leave the food and back out the door!"

Charley's voice cracked shrilly. "What door would that be?"

Lizzie glanced behind her. Although they hadn't taken more than a few steps into the cage, the door had disappeared. In its place were several hairy beings, gazing at them with obvious longing. It seemed likely that, if they weren't so large and Charley and Lizzie so comparatively small, they would have liked nothing more than to curl up in the girls' laps and go to sleep.

Despite the affectionate nature of the attack, Charley was fairly vibrating with panic by now.

"If only we could calm them down a bit..." she gibbered. "My mum always used to sing to me to calm me down when I was little, but now it's chocolate that does it. Course, I don't have any chocolate, do I? Not even a crumb." She said this last bit with real feeling.

"But that's it!" Lizzie would have clapped her hands if there had been any room for her to do it in. "Of course!" She gestured to the wall of creatures closing in on them from the front. "It's as plain as the nose on the face of that thing with the horns!"

Charley stared glumly at the thing with the horns. Its nose was the size of a two-litre bottle of cola. "It is?"

Lizzie grinned with excitement. Mrs Moscos wasn't the only person who was always telling her to think. And for once she had managed to follow this very sound advice. She knew that she was right.

"It's the humming, Charley," explained Lizzie. "That's why Boragian ramblers are so good as animal trainers. Because they hum all the time! It calms the creatures down!"

"Oh my gosh!" Charley couldn't have looked happier if Lizzie had just handed her a bar of chocolate. "Do you really think—"

Lizzie was not the most determined or decisive girl in the universe, but the possibility of being loved to death by a cage full of alien creatures transformed her. Without a second's hesitation, Lizzie started to hum.

The thing with the horns immediately slowed down, but the rest didn't seem to notice.

"Louder," urged Charley. "The ones at the back probably can't hear you."

Lizzie hummed louder and Charley joined in.

The pink gorilla with three eyes slowed down, as did the monkey-like creatures no bigger than a clothes peg, but the others all kept coming.

"Maybe they don't like the way we're humming," Charley suggested. "Maybe they'd like more of a song."

Lizzie sighed. Trust Charley to be critical, even at a time like this.

"We're not playing *Name That Tune*, you know," snapped Lizzie. All the same, she started to hum a song from school.

A few more creatures slowed their pace, and one or two even suddenly sat down, but the rest continued to drift towards them.

"Try something else," prodded Charley.

Lizzie bit her lip so she didn't say something she might regret. This was not the time to have a fight with Charley. She could fight with Charley later, when they were safely back at Park World.

"Tell you what," she said ever so sweetly. "Since you seem to be the expert, why don't *you* try something else?"

"All right." Charley's voice was also very sweet. "If that's the way you want to be, I will."

She raised her head and took a deep breath. Charley listened to the radio a great deal, and knew a lot of songs, but as she got ready to hum she forgot every song she knew except for one. And it wasn't even from the radio. It was from one of her favourite television commercials.

"Are you mad?" whispered Lizzie. "That's the Chocolate Snaps jingle." Which might, of course, have had something to do with Charley's choice.

Charley closed her eyes and kept humming. The Chocolate Snaps jingle always put the cat and the dog in the advert to sleep.

And it had the same effect on the alien mammals and whatever-remains. Within seconds, every one of them was sitting around them in a circle with its head cocked to one side.

"Come on! Let's feed them before they start wanting to be hugged again."

Lizzie moved to grab hold of the enormous bag of food they'd lugged in with them, but the silver tabby cat was asleep on her feet and she couldn't move.

"Wake up," called Lizzie. She gave it a gentle poke. The cat that really did look just like Rocky opened its eyes. "You have to move," Lizzie explained. She wiggled her foot. She looked over at Charley for a second, wondering if she was going to need some help, and when she looked down again the cat was gone. Lizzie stared at the spot where the cat had been, but all that was there now was some mud she must have picked up on her walk to the lake. There was no time, however, to dwell on the speed with which the cat had vanished. There was too much work to be done.

As things turned out, it was perhaps unfortunate that neither Lizzie nor Charley had much real experience of work. Lizzie sometimes had to load the dishwasher, and Charley was often called upon to lay the table for supper. But although they always complained about the unfairness of this slave labour, it was as arduous as a game of cards compared to hauling all the bags of food and jugs of water they needed into the cages. Indeed, after today, it was unlikely that either Lizzie or Charley would ever complain about laying the table again.

In films and books, people who are in the middle of an adventure in which they hold the fate of the universe in their hands don't usually fall asleep. But life doesn't always follow the same rules as films or books, and by the time Charley and Lizzie had fed and watered everything they were so exhausted that they collapsed in a heap on the floor outside the cages while they waited for the captive creatures to finish eating.

Charley's eyes started to close as though the lids were being pulled down by an outside force. "We have to get the creatures ready," she mumbled. "We don't have much time."

"I know..." murmured Lizzie. Her eyes too were being forced shut by something much stronger than she was. "We have to hurry..."

Charley didn't answer; she was already sound asleep.

Lizzie, however, didn't notice that Charley didn't answer. She was sound asleep too.

Lizzie Starts Thinking
Like Mrs Moscos

....

Lizzie and Charley might have slept for hours
if the ship hadn't dipped so suddenly and
sharply that they rolled across the cargo-hold.
It was hitting the wall on the other side that
woke them up.

Lizzie's first thought when she realized
she'd been sleeping was: Mrs Moscos is going
to kill me. Which was probably true. Mrs
Moscos was never that happy with Lizzie
when she was doing something right. This
time, however, even Lizzie could see that
falling asleep was the wrong thing to do.
Which is why, of course, it never happens
in books and films.

Lizzie's second thought was: What's that
noise?

She sat up quickly.

The noise in question, a low and steady hum, definitely wasn't coming from any of the cages.

Charley also sat up, rubbing her eyes. "What's that?"

"I don't know." Lizzie laughed, trying to convince herself that nothing too awful was happening. "Maybe the ship's rocking a bit. You know, the way ships do." As far as she remembered, the rowing boat had rocked the whole time.

"Rocking a bit?" Charley frowned. "It felt to me like we fell through a hole."

"Fell through a hole?" Lizzie laughed, though somewhat nervously. "It was probably just a wave."

But Charley was wide awake now. "I don't think you can get waves in jelly," she said. "Or holes." She met Lizzie's eyes. "What's that purring sound?"

Because she really didn't like being blamed when things went wrong, Lizzie normally went on fibbing until she could fib no more.

But not this time. It was almost as though Mrs Moscos could still see and hear her, forcing Lizzie to tell the truth. "It's not purring." Lizzie sighed, suddenly feeling compelled to be as honest and practical as Mrs Moscos herself. "I think it must be the engines."

"The engines? Oh my gosh, they're starting the engines. We have to hurry!" Acting on her own words, Charley scrambled to her feet. "Come on, Lizzie. The Weis are getting ready to leave—"

Lizzie's new compulsion to be practical and honest continued. "No they're not," she cut in. "They've already left."

"You what?" Charley's eyes grew even wider. "I don't believe this!" Charley moaned, causing several of the captive creatures to look up with some concern.

"You don't have to make it sound like it's all *my* fault, you know," protested Lizzie.

Charley glared. "Well, whose fault is it, then? Mrs Moscos told you to listen for the engines starting, didn't she? She didn't say *after* you'd had a nap—"

"You fell asleep too." Lizzie glared back. "And, anyway, I reckon we took off sooner than Mrs Moscos expected. She probably wasn't even back from her shopping yet."

Charley moaned again. "So now what?" she demanded. "We don't even have the sunglasses so Mrs Moscos can tell us what to do next."

Normally, Lizzie never thought like anyone else, but now she found herself wondering what Mrs Moscos would do. What would Mrs Moscos tell us to do? she asked herself. What would Mrs Moscos tell us to do? The answer came to her as clearly as if Mrs Moscos herself had spoken: they didn't need the glasses. What they needed was a radio transmitter – any old transmitter that happened to be lying around the ship. It stood to reason. Until they could contact Mrs Moscos, they had no way of knowing where she was, or when she would be ready.

"We don't need the glasses," said Lizzie. "We can talk to Mrs Moscos without them."

"Oh, really?" Charley raised one eyebrow. "And just how do you plan to do that? Use your psychic powers?"

"No," said Lizzie. "I plan to use the transmitter in the control room."

Charley's laugh was a bitter one. "Oh, well, that's all right, then, isn't it? We just stroll into the control room and ask that nice captain if we can use his radio to call our friend! I'm sure he won't mind."

Lizzie hadn't yet worked out all the details of precisely *how* they would get access to the ship's transmitter but, once again, the answer came to Lizzie as though Mrs Moscos were still in contact with her through the radio in the sunglasses.

Lizzie smiled confidently. "Then we'll have to take over the ship, won't we?"

"Take over the ship," Charley repeated. She stared at Lizzie in a way that suggested nothing in the universe would ever surprise her again. "You really have lost your mind, haven't you? It may have escaped your attention, Lizzie Wesson, but we're slightly outnumbered by armed Wei soldiers. You know, like three hundred to one."

Lizzie stared back. She agreed that their chances of successfully overpowering the Weis weren't enormous, but the alternative – doing nothing – seemed to her to be guaranteed to fail.

"And what's your better idea? Go to Wei and spend the rest of our lives mucking out Louis Wu's zoo?"

The look on Charley's face clearly said that growing old on Wei wasn't an idea that appealed to her any more than it appealed to Lizzie.

"But surely Mrs Moscos wouldn't abandon us," Charley argued. "Maybe if we just wait—"

"Haven't you got all your memory back yet?" demanded Lizzie. "Mrs Moscos is always abandoning us. She abandoned us on Wei. She abandoned us on the uncharted asteroid in the tail of the forgotten galaxy. Anyway, we don't have time to wait. If I'm right and we left before she'd finished her shopping, she doesn't even know where we are. Our only chance is to get back into radio contact with her."

"Don't you think you've overlooked something sort of crucial?" asked Charley. "Unless they die laughing, the Weis aren't going to be too threatened by us in our yellow anoraks and red noses."

Lizzie smiled. She definitely felt that she was starting to get the hang of this hero business. "They will if we have an army behind us."

"An army?" Charley spluttered. "And where are we going to get an ar—" She broke off, suddenly aware of the scores of eyes watching them from behind glass walls. "Oh, you can't be serious…" She turned back to Lizzie. "Are you suggesting that we use the creatures as an army? After all the trouble we had calming them down, you want to let them all out?"

"All right," said Lizzie. "What's your better idea?"

Lizzie and Charley Take Their First Steps Towards a Military Career

....

In Lizzie's opinion, her plan was so simple, sensible and totally brilliant that even she was a little surprised that she'd thought of it. They knew the Weis were afraid of the creatures and couldn't handle them. So if they led the creatures to the control room they were bound to cause panic and confusion. Lizzie reckoned that the Weis would be far too busy trying to stop the creatures from running amok on the ship to pay any attention to two Boragian ramblers. Indeed, Lizzie doubted that Mrs Moscos could come up with as good a plan, though this was not a statement she would be likely to make in Mrs Moscos's hearing.

Charley, however, was less enthusiastic. This was typical of Charley. She could never just say, "Great! That's a terrific idea! Let's go for it!" She always had to find fault.

While Lizzie busily opened each cage, Charley followed her from one to the other, voicing her objections to her plan the whole time. What if they couldn't find the control room? What if the Weis shot them? What if the Weis locked themselves in the control room? What if everything went exactly according to Lizzie's plan, but when it came to it they couldn't work the transmitter? Charley didn't think that a person who had difficulty in finding her favourite radio station would necessarily be able to work an alien transmitter.

Only when she had opened all three cages did Lizzie turn her attention to Charley. "What if we're suddenly captured by space pirates with four heads and baseball bats for arms?" she demanded. "What then?"

Charley didn't blink. "Frankly, considering the day we've been having, it wouldn't surprise me in the least." She folded her arms across her chest. "And that doesn't answer my other questions."

"I'm not going to answer your other questions," Lizzie informed her. "I'm going to take over the control room and use the transmitter." She said this so confidently that you'd think she could find her favourite radio station without any trouble. "The only question I'm interested in is are you coming with me or are you staying here?"

Charley cast another wary glance at the watching eyes surrounding them. The Weis weren't the only ones who were afraid of the creatures. It was true that they seemed very affectionate, but it was also true that, with the exception of the tabby cat, they all looked like something out of her worst nightmares.

On the other hand, as little as Charley liked the idea of taking over the control room with an army of space creatures, she liked the idea of being left on her own in the cargo-hold even less.

Charley sighed. "I'm coming with you. But I want you to know that if anything goes wrong, Lizzie Wesson, I'm holding you personally responsible."

Since this wasn't exactly a newsflash, Lizzie wasn't even listening. She was standing straight and tall the way soldiers do in the movies. Indeed, she felt as if she were in a film – a war film in which she was very definitely the hero. She was General Lizzie Wesson, and she was ready for action. She gazed at her troops, all of whom gazed back at her placidly – many from several eyes. She raised one hand. "All right, men," Lizzie shouted. She faced the door. "Forward! March!"

And in this film, Charley's role was clearly that of reporter. "They're not moving," said Charley.

Lizzie looked round. Charley was right. The creatures were all exactly where they were before she gave her command.

"Maybe they don't understand English," suggested Charley. "Maybe we should be humming."

Lizzie shook her head. "It was the humming that made them relax in the first place. It's not going to make them leave their cages."

Charley spread her arms in exasperation. "Well, what then? We can't just stand—"

"Do that again," ordered Lizzie.

"Pardon?" Charley looked at her as though she wasn't sure Lizzie was speaking to her. "Do what again?"

"Open your arms. Some of them started moving. Maybe they thought you wanted to hug them."

"Hug them?"

Lizzie sighed impatiently. "You don't *really* have to hug them. You just have to make them think that's what you want to do." She patted Charley's shoulder. "Encourage them, that's all. Make them come to you."

Dozens of eyes, some of them flashing, watched Charley intently. She couldn't help feeling that she was the one who needed encouragement. She took a deep breath, and once more opened her arms out wide.

"Go on!" urged Lizzie.

This was obviously all the encouragement Charley was going to get at the moment. She took a deep breath, shut her eyes tightly, and once more opened her arms wide.

"It's working!" Lizzie spread her arms as well. "Come on!" she pleaded. "Come to Lizzie and Charley!"

Charley risked a look. The creatures were all jamming the doorways, eager to get out and be embraced.

"How could the Weis want to turn them into handbags and pet food?" asked Lizzie. "Look at them. All they want is love." She tugged Charley forward. "You keep facing them with your arms open and I'll guide you to the door."

It wasn't until they reached the door that

Lizzie noticed that it didn't have a handle, which made her hesitate with confusion for a second.

With her unerring instinct for disaster, Charley glanced over her shoulder. "What's wrong? You can't get it open?"

"Of course I can open it." Lizzie laughed with relief. "It opens by touch. Remember?"

Charley pointed out that it didn't seem to open by touch.

Lizzie put her hand against the door again, but still nothing happened.

"Maybe it's stuck," offered Charley.

Lizzie scowled. "Thank you for pointing that out, Charlene." She braced herself and gave the door a thump, and then another. Lizzie took a deep breath and was just about to throw her shoulder against the stubborn door when Charley screamed.

It was an urgent sort of scream. Lizzie turned round. The creatures who were out of their cages had started to rush towards her eagerly, pushed forward by the equally eager creatures behind them. The reason they weren't rushing towards Charley was because Charley was nowhere in sight. Lizzie was so surprised that she might very well have been trampled if Charley hadn't reached out from the store cupboard and yanked her to safety.

"Maybe it isn't going to be as easy to control them as you thought," Charley grunted.

Lizzie bristled with indignation. "I just haven't totally got the hang of it yet, that's all." She peered round the door of the cupboard just in time to see her army, carried forward by its own momentum, steaming into the stubborn door. The metal groaned and crumbled under its force.

"Well, at least they got the door open," commented Charley.

Not slowed down in the slightest, the creatures kept going, trampling the door under their feet.

Lizzie sighed. Maybe it wasn't going to be as easy to control them as she'd thought.

But then she remembered the options if her plan didn't work – spending the rest of her life working in Louis Wu's safari park, or execution – and her resolve strengthened. She had to try.

"Come on!" Lizzie pulled Charley out of the cupboard with her. "We've got to get at the front so we can lead them to the control room."

The rather nervous expression Charley had been wearing since nearly being mown down by the affectionate aliens turned to one of amazement. "You remember how to get back to the control room?" She sounded impressed.

It was rare for Lizzie to impress Charley in a positive way. She didn't want to ruin this moment by admitting that she hadn't a clue how to get back to the control room.

"I think so," Lizzie answered with so much confidence that it was if she had said "yes". "Now come on. We don't have time to waste."

Despite the fact that it was only the odd limb, foot, hand or face that bore any resemblance to anything human, freedom affected the captive creatures in much the way that freedom affects people. When they realized that they were no longer imprisoned, they became jubilant and excited. They screeched with joy and roared with pleasure. They charged down the corridor as though it would lead them all home.

Unfortunately, this enthusiasm made it even more difficult to get ahead of the creatures.

"We're never going to get through," gasped Charley. "They're *everywhere*."

Which was true enough. They flew, they rolled, they ran, they hopped, they jumped, they slithered up the walls and along the ground – they were above Lizzie and Charley, below them, and on every side.

Trying very hard not to tread on anything, Lizzie squeezed through the horde. This was possible when the creatures in question were the same size as the girls and relatively compact. When the creatures in question were large and unwieldy, however, forcing their way past extra arms, legs, heads or tails was no easier than pushing a camel through the eye of a needle.

"Is it me," panted Charley, "or is this not working very well?"

Despite the setbacks of her campaign so far, Lizzie was still into her role as military leader. From what she could remember from movies, generals never told their troops how bad things were, in case it lowered their morale. For this reason, Lizzie was not prepared to admit that things weren't going precisely to plan.

"We're doing all right," gasped Lizzie. "At least we're moving." Though it would have been better if she had some idea as to where.

Finally fed up with trying to squeeze past a big, shimmering wing, Lizzie dropped to her knees and started to crawl under it instead.

Charley dropped to her knees too. "So what happens if we can't find the control room?" she asked as she followed Lizzie over an extremely large claw.

Lizzie never had the chance to answer. For at that moment they finally broke through the front of the army, and Charley's question proved unneccesary.

"Good grief!" gasped Charley. "They found the control room."

Indeed, straight ahead of them was the purple door with the silver Wei symbol for flight on it.

Lizzie was so pleased by this piece of luck that she quickly took credit for it. "Didn't I tell you I'd find it?" she crowed.

Charley glanced warily over her shoulder. They were only a few metres from the control room door, but the creatures were still moving forward. "You'd better stop them," she hissed.

But it was already too late. Lizzie and Charley just had time to flatten themselves against the wall as the captive creatures bounded across the short distance between them and the door. And then, as was their custom, knocked down the door and continued right over it.

Charley's look was as scathing as possible considering that she had a hairy yellow tail in her face. "Maybe you should've worked out how to get them to stop before you let them out of their cages," she said.

From Certain Angles, Things Couldn't Have Worked Out Better if Lizzie Really Had Planned Them

....

To say that the Wei command was surprised to see Lizzie, Charley and the hundreds of captive creatures would be something of an understatement. The Weis were accustomed to being obeyed and to being in control. Nothing like this had ever happened on a Wei ship before, and the captain and his crew certainly hadn't expected it to happen on their ship. Indeed, the Weis were so surprised that for several seconds they did nothing. They simply stayed where they were, staring at the doorway as though they didn't believe their eyes.

In those several seconds the mood of the creatures changed from one of jubilation to one of rage as they recognized their captors. Feathers ruffled, and hair stood on end. Many of the birds were in the lead, and they swiftly rose into the air while their comrades charged towards the Wei command as though it were the meal they'd been waiting for for so long. They growled, they barked, they gurgled, they roared, they whistled and they yelped – indeed, they made every animal sound that the girls had ever heard, and several dozen more.

"Good grief!" gasped Charley as she and Lizzie peered round the doorway. "They really don't like the Weis, do they?"

Lizzie couldn't believe their luck. The Wei captain and his crew were trapped. There was no way they could stop the charging creatures, never mind make a break for safety and get out of the room.

"What do you think about that?" Lizzie shouted above the uproar. She gave Charley a soldierly whack on the shoulder. "We've captured our first prisoners." If that wasn't heroic, Lizzie didn't know what was. Things couldn't have worked out better if she really had planned them this way.

But then again, perhaps they could have.

For at that moment, the Wei captain shouted, "Burntgreensanddicedribbons!" and in the next moment two things happened. The first was that a shrill, pulsating alarm began to sound through the ship. The second was that a transparent dome dropped from the ceiling to surround the command centre – just in time for the attacking creatures to hit it at full tilt.

Unfortunately, the dome, unlike the doors, did not buckle and break. It was the animals at the front that collapsed.

There was such a din as the creatures all screeched and howled in panic and distress, that neither Lizzie nor Charley would have heard the heavy footsteps rushing towards them if there hadn't been so many of them.

They seemed to echo from every level of the ship.

Charley stood there with her mouth open in a silent scream, and her eyes as large as dinner plates.

"Come on," Lizzie ordered. "We've got to get the creatures out of here before we're trapped. Then we can double back later."

Panic was making Charley exceedingly testy. "What do you mean, 'before we're trapped'? We're on a ship in the middle of space, Lizzie. We're already trapped." She moaned out loud. "This is it, isn't it? It's all over except for the part where they execute us."

"Don't be ridiculous," Lizzie snapped back. She was beginning to sound like Mrs Moscos as well as think like her. "This is a setback, not defeat. They haven't beaten us yet."

"Oh, really? And how do you work that out?" Charley demanded. "You couldn't stop them. How are you going to get them to follow us out again?"

"Hum," said Lizzie. It was amazing how good she was getting at being logical and reasonable in such a Mrs Moscos sort of way. "Hum loudly."

Once again, the humming of the Chocolate Snaps jingle acted as a tranquillizer. Some of the creatures were dazed from crashing into the dome, and all of them were still agitated, but they calmed down enough to see Lizzie and Charley edging backwards through the doorway, their arms spread wide.

And, also once again, they started to follow. "You see?"

But Charley did not return Lizzie's smile. There were three different corridors leading from the control room, and Charley was frantically looking from one to the next. "Which way?" she wailed.

Since the approaching footsteps seemed to be coming from every direction, Lizzie couldn't see that it really mattered which way they went, but a good general, of course, tries not to worry her troops if possible, so Lizzie shouted, "That way!" with great certainty, and started running down the corridor to the left.

Once again, luck seemed to be on Lizzie's side. They reached the end of the first corridor, the second corridor and the third without any sign of a Wei soldier.

"It should be safe to double back soon," decided Lizzie.

And then they turned into the fourth corridor.

Lizzie stopped so abruptly that Charley walked right into her.

"I knew it!" wailed Charley. "I knew it was too good to last."

Coming towards them was a Wei soldier.

"Charley!" hissed Lizzie. "Charley, look who it is! It's the soldier who took our sunglasses." She could see them poking out from his pocket.

"And what?" Charley hissed back. "You think that's good?"

Indeed, Lizzie did think it was fairly good. "If we can get our glasses back it is."

"That's a great plan." Charley's fingers closed around Lizzie's arm. "Except for the fact that he's the one with the gun."

Not only was the soldier the one with the gun, but he was pointing his gun at Lizzie, Charley and the captive creatures.

"Banglesummersloop!" boomed the soldier, raising his weapon. "Banglesummersloopoverstraw!"

It wasn't so much what he said as the way he said it that made them all stop.

The soldier took aim.

Lizzie and Charley closed their eyes. Lizzie knew that if she really were a hero in a movie this was the moment when she would suddenly pull a machine-gun and several grenades from her pocket and wipe out every Wei soldier on the ship. But Lizzie, of course, was not a movie hero but a small girl who'd never been given so much as a water pistol because her parents didn't believe in violence. So when she closed her eyes she didn't imagine blowing the soldier to pieces with a large automatic weapon. Instead, she imagined a baby grand piano falling gently from the sky to pin the soldier down so that he couldn't shoot them.

"If we don't survive this, Lizzie," said Charley in a wobbly voice, "I want you to know that even though this is all your fault, you're still the best friend I've ever had."

"Me too," Lizzie whispered back.

There was an ear-piercing scream, a terrible thud, and then the sound of quite a few piano keys being hit simultaneously.

"Lizzie? Lizzie, are you still there?"

Lizzie moved her toes, then her fingers, then her head. She seemed to still be there. "Yes." She opened one eye. "Oh my gosh! Charley, look! We've been saved."

By, curiously enough, a baby grand piano that looked exactly like the one in the Wessons' living room, even down to the ring mark where Lizzie once left a cup of tea.

Charley opened her eyes. The Wei soldier was unconscious beneath the piano, passed out from the shock.

"What's your piano doing here?" asked Charley.

It was a very good question, but not one that Lizzie felt like trying to answer at the moment. Hurtling down the corridor behind the unconscious Wei soldier were several extremely conscious ones.

"Never mind that now." Lizzie drew Charley's attention to the conscious soldiers. "We've got to get out of here. Fast." She started to run, the glasses forgotten.

"Well, I'm certainly glad *you* think this is being saved," said Charley, racing after her.

Things Are Always Dark Before They Get Darker

···

Neither Lizzie nor Charley was particularly
known for her physical skills, unless you
counted shopping as an indoor sport.
Charley was so bad at PE that she was always
the last person picked for teams, and Lizzie
was just lazy. She couldn't, for instance, see
any point in riding a bicycle when you could
take a bus, or charging across a hockey field
when you could walk at a leisurely pace and
not get all sweaty. It would therefore have
surprised those who knew them best to see
the speed with which Charley and Lizzie –
devotedly followed by their affectionate army
– raced down the corridor to their right and
disappeared round the next turning before
the conscious Wei soldiers reached their
stricken comrade.

"We did it!" crowed Lizzie. She came to a stop, leaning against the wall to catch her breath. "They can't get at us, not with all the creatures between us."

Charley collapsed beside her. "But what about contacting Mrs Moscos?" she gasped. "How are we going to get to the sunglasses or the transmitter now?"

This, of course, was another extremely good question – and one that Lizzie was luckily saved from having to answer by the sudden sound of purring.

Lizzie looked down. Sitting at her feet was the silver tabby cat that looked like Rocky. Although far less alarming than everything else that was happening, the way the silver tabby seemed to go into and come out of thin air was definitely a puzzle.

"Where did you come from?" asked Lizzie.

As if in answer, the tabby began to purr even more loudly.

"Shhh…" cautioned Lizzie. "You're making too much noise."

The silver tabby reacted as though Lizzie had told him to step up the volume.

"Make him shut up!" begged Charley. "The whole ship's going to hear him."

"He's just upset, that's all. Aren't you, boy?"

"So am I," hissed Charley as the purring grew even louder. "Do something quick!"

The only thing Lizzie could think to do was pick the cat up. It had always worked when Rocky was upset.

Lizzie leaned down and scooped the silver tabby into her arms. Which was when she saw what was underneath the cat.

"Charley!" She gave Charley a nudge. "Charley, look what he was sitting on!"

"Good grief!" Charley laughed out loud. "It's our sunglasses!"

Lizzie looked from the sunglasses to the cat. Besides the question of how the cat had suddenly materialized like that, there was the even more interesting question of how their sunglasses – last seen in the pocket of the unfortunate Wei soldier – had ended up beneath him. Though now, of course, was not the time to give either question a great deal of thought.

Holding the silver tabby with one hand, Lizzie retrieved the sunglasses from the floor. "We've got to find out how to get out of here." She handed Charley a pair of sunglasses. "Quick, put them on."

For a change, Charley didn't argue but did exactly as she was told. "Good grief," she cried. "I feel like I've gone blind."

Charley had a point. Although the visibility through the sunglasses had always been limited, it was now non-existent. Lizzie squinted through the lenses into what might have been an extremely dark night. Except for a faint, red glow very close to her face she couldn't see even the shadows she'd been able to see through the glasses before.

"Can you see your nose shining?" asked Lizzie.

"I think so."

"Then you haven't gone blind." Lizzie took off her glasses. The corridor was still as black as pitch. "The lights have gone out."

"Really?" Charley pushed her glasses up on her forehead. "What do you think's going on? Do you think it's some sort of trap?"

"I doubt it," Lizzie assured her. After all, the Weis had been thrown into confusion and panic; they weren't likely to be laying traps. "They probably turned them off to calm down the creatures," she reasoned. "You know, like they did in the cargo-hold."

Lizzie definitely considered this another piece of good luck. Throwing the animals into darkness to make them more mellow hadn't worked in the cargo-hold, so there was no reason to suppose that it would work any better in the body of the ship. All the lack of light would do was slow down the Weis.

Charley, however, didn't share Lizzie's optimism. Not being able to see properly always made her uneasy – but especially so on a Wei ship.

"I just hope you're right, and they're not coming after us."

But Lizzie was feeling far too pleased with herself to be bothered by something as minor as a power failure. What was her idea of letting the creatures run amok on the ship if it wasn't genius?

"They can't be coming after us," Lizzie assured her. "There were hundreds of captive creatures between us and those soldiers, and it's not going to be any easier to get round or through them in the dark."

"But what if the soldiers shoot them?" fretted Charley. "Then there won't be anything between them and us."

"They're not going to shoot them." Lizzie put on her sunglasses again. "Don't you remember what Mrs Moscos said? Louis Wu will have their heads if they don't bring the creatures safely back to Wei. I reckon that includes shooting them as well as letting them die of neglect."

But Charley was now in the mood to

worry. "I can't hear anything," she said once she'd put on her own sunglasses. "Maybe that soldier did something to them. Maybe they're not working any more."

Lizzie didn't hear anything either, but since she now considered herself to be a girl of determination, logic and practical action, she simply tapped the nose bridge and said, "Mrs Moscos? Come in, Mrs Moscos," in the voice of someone accustomed to being in difficult situations and surviving.

There was a swarming of static, and then – to both Charley's and Lizzie's immense relief – Mrs Moscos replied, sounding quite annoyed.

"Well, I must say it is about time." Mrs Moscos's voice crackled through the stars, a sound that reminded at least one of the girls of a chocolate wrapper being opened. "I was beginning to think that something had gone wrong."

Hunger made Charley's reply a bit sharper than she intended because she had just remembered how hungry she was.

"Something did go wrong," she said.
"The Wei ship took off with us still on it,
didn't it?"

Lizzie kicked her in the shin. If Mrs
Moscos had forgotten that that wasn't the
plan, she didn't see why Charley should
remind her.

Mrs Moscos, however, seemed to be in
a more philosophical mood than usual.
"It would have been nice if you could have
managed to stay awake, but there was a great
deal of work to do. And the ship would have
left when it did in any event, of course, and
I would still have been purchasing our
supplies, so – as with most human endeavour
– it didn't really make any difference in the
end."

"You mean you *knew* all along?" It seemed
to Lizzie that Mrs Moscos might have
warned them that this might happen *before*
they got on the ship as opposed to telling
them after.

"And why would I do that?" demanded Mrs Moscos, who apparently could read Lizzie's mind even when they were light-years apart. "It would have been completely counter-productive. It was imperative that you be on board. Neither of you would have got on the ship if you knew it was about to depart – and then where would we be?"

"I'll tell you where we wouldn't be," grumbled Charley. "We wouldn't be hiding from the Weis in deepest space, that's for sure."

Mrs Moscos agreed with her. "Precisely. And some of the greatest treasures of the cosmos would have been lost for ever as a result."

"They may still be lost if you don't tell us how to get out of here," said Lizzie.

Mrs Moscos sighed. "Worry, worry, worry..." she chanted. "As it happens, Lizzie Wesson, nothing could be easier. Certainly not this side of Luga Belosi."

Charley had been half listening to Mrs

Moscos, and half listening to the rumblings her stomach had been making since it remembered the existence of chocolate elsewhere in the universe, but now a different sound caught her attention. It seemed to be coming from the walls.

"English!" squeaked Charley. "They're speaking in English over the tannoy!"

"Is that so?" asked Mrs Moscos. "And what are they saying?"

"They're saying they have us surrounded," Lizzie reported.

Mrs Moscos took this announcement in her stride. "Ah," she said. "They must have worked out that you are not Boragian ramblers after all. You will have to stop the gabbing and move quickly."

"Move where?" Lizzie was shrill with frustration. "You haven't told us what to do yet."

"Perhaps because I believed that was fairly obvious," replied Mrs Moscos. Her voice was as warm as an ice-cube. "Now that you have made contact I can pinpoint precisely where you are. Indeed, your ship is already visible on my long-distance viewer. All you have to do is gather together the creatures."

"Oh, is that all?" Lizzie's laugh was hollow. "*Just* gather them together."

"Precisely. I shall be with you by the time you have done that, but just to be on the very safe side, count down from twenty before you activate the transporter."

"But Mrs Moscos—" Charley began.

"Less talk and more walk!" called Mrs Moscos, and her voice vanished in a buzz of static.

Not having Mrs Moscos to argue with, Charley turned to Lizzie. "You do realize that this is really bad news, don't you?" she demanded. "How are we meant to gather them together when they're running all over the place and the lights are out?"

Lizzie sighed. It really was astounding how everything always ended up being her fault. "We'll just have to move about humming, won't we? It's the only way they'll be able to find us."

"And what if the Weis find us?"

"The Weis won't find us," said Lizzie. "They're not going to be wandering round in the dark, are they? They might bump into a three-headed lizard."

Which made Lizzie wrong on three counts.

A voice that didn't come from the sunglasses but from alarmingly near by suddenly shouted in English, "Look! Shiny red noses! Do you think that's them?"

And a second voice, also speaking perfect English, said, "Well, they certainly aren't reindeer."

More Fun than a Ship Full of Endangered Life Forms

....

There was no time for Lizzie and Charley to remove their noses and scuttle away in the dark, because no sooner did the soldiers find them than the lights came back on.

"Good grief!" whispered Charley. "We're surrounded."

Besides the two Weis who spoke such excellent English, there were another two at the other end of the corridor, all of them pointing their weapons at Lizzie and Charley in a serious way.

"Well, well, well..." said the taller of the first pair of soldiers. "If it isn't two of the most wanted outlaws in Wei history. The captain will be very delighted to see *you*."

The second soldier smiled. Neither Lizzie nor Charley remembered ever seeing a Wei smile before, but they both hoped fervently that they would never see it again.

"Louis Wu will be even happier," said the second soldier. He glanced at his comrade. "Perhaps the captain will not be the only one to get a promotion out of this."

Lizzie could feel Charley looking at her. And she knew what Charley was thinking. Charley was thinking that this was all Lizzie's fault. Why hadn't Lizzie thought to take off the luminous noses so they wouldn't be seen in the dark? Why had she insisted on leaving the snack bar? Why didn't she do something?

Lizzie didn't know why she hadn't remembered about the noses, and she didn't know why she'd been so insistent about visiting the sailing ship, but she reckoned that there was something she could do. It wasn't much, but it was worth a try.

"Pardon me," said Lizzie, using her very

best manners, "but I'm afraid you've made a mistake. We're not two of the most wanted outlaws in the history of Wei. We're just simple Boragian ramblers."

Charley nodded enthusiastically. "That's true. That's absolutely true. We're just simple Boragian ramblers who happen to speak English."

"Are you indeed?" The second soldier removed a piece of paper from his jacket and held it out for them to see. "Then who might these be?"

It was a photograph of Lizzie and Charley, apparently taken from a Wei ship since they were looking straight up with rather shocked expressions on their faces.

"Good grief!" breathed Charley.

"It must be the poster Mrs Moscos told us about," Lizzie whispered.

A single word was written in Wei above the photograph, and several more Wei words were written below it.

The first soldier pointed his gun at the

single word at the top of the paper. *"Digglemop,"* he read. "Wanted," he kindly translated. He pointed his gun at the several words underneath the picture. "Take alive. Troublesome but not armed."

Troublesome? Lizzie thought that was a bit much. If anyone was troublesome, it was the Weis, not her and Charley.

The soldier put the poster back in his jacket, then turned his gun on two of the most wanted outlaws in the history of Wei. "Move!" he ordered. "The captain very anxiously awaits you."

Lizzie glanced down so she didn't trip over the silver tabby, but once again the cat had vanished.

"I did mean today," barked the soldier.

Lizzie and Charley did as they were told, keeping their eyes straight ahead as they followed the Weis. They could hear the creatures roaring and thudding about in other corridors, but the way to the control room was depressingly clear.

The Weis weren't masters of a great deal of the universe just because they were mean, greedy and unpleasant. They were efficient and well organized as well. In the short time that Charley and Lizzie had been away from the control room, order had been restored and the broken door replaced with a glass one. Presumably the new door was of the same unbending glass as the dome, which was no longer in view.

The captain stood up as Lizzie and Charley and their escorts entered.

"Ah, if it isn't the troublesome girls from Earth!" he boomed. "My promotion has arrived!" Neither Lizzie nor Charley had suspected that the Wei captain was capable of looking happy, but he obviously was – although not in a way that was in any danger of becoming contagious. "Come in, come in!" he urged, as if they had a choice. "So nice of you to drop by!"

He sat them across from him in the command centre where he could keep a constant eye on them. "I do not want anything to happen to you two," the captain assured them. "I am not letting you out of my vision until I hand you over to Louis Wu himself."

Which, apparently, was something he intended to do as soon as possible. Once Charley and Lizzie were in their seats, it was all systems go in the command room. The captain barked orders into the sound system, fired all engines, and cranked up the speed of the ship as far as it would go.

"Don't look so gloomy," Lizzie whispered to Charley. "We're not beaten yet."

"We're not?" Charley's eyes were round with innocence, but her voice was sharp with sarcasm. "You mean we're really the ones in control and the Weis are *our* prisoners? Don't you think we should tell them that?"

"No, really," Lizzie insisted. "Think about it. They're not going to execute us, right? They have to take us alive."

Charley looked at her out of the corner

-187-

of one eye. "And that's what? Something to cheer me up?"

"Of course it is. Since we're alive, and they have to keep us that way, we still have a chance of getting free, don't we?"

This made total sense to Lizzie.

But not to Charley.

"No," said Charley. She said this firmly. "We don't still have a chance of getting free. We have much more chance of joining the Wei army." Her eyes darted round them. There were quite a few members of that organization in the control room. "Which is practically what we've done."

"You have to listen to me, Charley." Her eyes on the captain and his crew, Lizzie leaned closer. "I have a plan."

"Really? Is it as good as your last plan?"

Lizzie generously decided to ignore Charley's sarcasm. After all, it had been quite a day. And it must be well past Charley's suppertime by now. Charley was never at her best and brightest when she missed meals.

"It's better. It solves all our problems at one go."

Charley's face seemed to be permanently frozen in a sour expression. "You mean we wake up and discover this has all been a ghastly dream?"

"No, I mean we get all the creatures outside the control room, and then we transport us all to safety."

"And what are the Weis going to be doing while we're doing that?" Charley enquired. "Just standing about, waving goodbye?"

"The Weis are a little busy right now." Half the crew was still dealing with the rampaging creatures, and the other half was rushing about the control room trying to get them to Wei as quickly as possible. "With any luck, we can get to the doorway without them noticing."

"And how are you planning to get all the creatures to the doorway? Or is that a detail you've overlooked?"

Lizzie was rather pleased that, for once,

she hadn't overlooked anything. "That's the beauty of my plan. Look around, Charley. We're in the one place in the ship that actually makes it easy to get the creatures to come to us."

Charley looked around, but all she saw were Wei soldiers. "I hope I'm missing something," she said, "because all I see are a lot of things that make calling them pretty hard."

"You're not looking in the right place." Lizzie nodded at the console in front of them. "Look there. What do you see?"

"Buttons, and lights, and dials, and—" Charley broke off as her eyes fell on the rectangle of chrome that looked very much like her mother's cheese grater at home. "Oh," she said. "And a microphone."

"What'd I tell you?" crowed Lizzie. "No matter where they are, the creatures will hear the humming and come. And as soon as we see them outside, we make a dash for the door, I activate the transporter, and we're out of here." What could be simpler than that?

"Hang on!" The sudden look of hope that had appeared on Charley's face disappeared again just as quickly. "The captain's not going to let us use the microphone, is he?"

"Well, not if he knows that we're using it he won't." Lizzie made an effort not to smile. If the Weis saw her smiling they might wonder why. "But he's not going to know, is he? I watched him. That yellow button switches it on. So all I have to do is push that, and then we lean forward a bit and hum."

Charley didn't like performing in public. It was bad enough when the public was your friends and family, but it seemed to Charley that it took on a new dimension of horror when the public was the command of a Wei spaceship.

"Oh, please… There's nothing to worry about." Lizzie stretched her arms and yawned, as a person does on long-distance flights. "They're not going to hear us over the racket they're making. And the Weis in the

rest of the ship will think it's the captain."
Her finger fell on the yellow button.

Charley didn't argue any more. One eye on
the captain, and one eye on the glass door,
she and Lizzie leaned into the console and
softly but steadily started to hum the
Chocolate Snaps jingle.

Hummed slowly and softly, the Chocolate
Snaps jingle proved to be very relaxing.
Charley had almost succeeded in putting
herself to sleep when Lizzie yelped.

"What happened?" Charley sat up straight,
blinking.

"Look who's here!" Lizzie's eyes were on
the floor.

Charley looked down. Sound asleep at
Lizzie's feet was the silver tabby. "Good grief.
How did he get in here?"

This, however, was yet another question
that was not to be answered.

Lizzie grabbed her wrist. "Charley!" she
hissed. "Look, it's working. Look at the
door!"

The several heads of the starbat of Qui were peering through the glass.

Even as Charley and Lizzie watched, more heads appeared beside, above and under the starbat.

"Right." Lizzie casually reached over and turned off the tannoy. "Let's get out of here." She scooped up the silver tabby so that he wouldn't be left behind, and rose to her feet.

It has to be said that, from this point on, Lizzie's plan had not been worked through properly. She vaguely thought that they would reach the door so quickly that the Weis wouldn't see them until it was too late. She vaguely thought that they would have the element of surprise on their side.

What she hadn't thought of was the possibility that the Wei captain would notice what they were doing before they took more than a few steps.

"What's going on?" shouted the captain. "Where did that cat come from?"

Lizzie's mother was nothing like the Wei

captain, but when Lizzie's mother asked her a question she didn't particularly want to answer, Lizzie always asked a question in return, and that was what she did now.

"What?" Lizzie smiled innocently, inching her way towards the door.

The captain did not return her smile. "Get back to your seats immediately!" he bellowed.

"We just want to stretch our legs," said Lizzie, still smiling and inching. "We've—"

Lizzie never finished explaining that she and Charley had been sitting for quite a while and their feet were going numb. The captain's eyes fell on the new glass door for the first time – and on what was behind it.

"Cellosoverdusseldorf!" he yelled. "Cellosoverdusseldorf! Cellosoverdusseldorf!"

The ship's crew was one of the best in the universe. To a Wei, they turned at the sound of their captain's voice, and instantly took in the situation. Their response time was quick as an electron; they moved to act.

The creature that the Weis feared most in all the cosmos was the two-toed dragon of Soo. They had been under the impression that they had killed every two-toed dragon that ever existed, but they were now proved wrong.

A two-toed dragon the colour of pond scum and as large as an elephant suddenly rose up between the starship command and two of the most wanted outlaws in the history of Wei, howling and thudding its tail to show that it was in quite a bad mood.

Charley's fingers dug into Lizzie's arm. She couldn't get over their misfortune. Now they were going to be eaten by a mythical beast. "Good grief!" she squeaked. "Just when you think things can't get any worse, they get really really bad!"

There was nothing the Weis could do. They couldn't attack the dragon without the risk of hitting Lizzie and Charley, but if they didn't attack the dragon, the dragon might attack the girls. Either way, the great Louis Wu was going to be in an even worse mood than the dragon was.

"Come over to safety!" shouted the captain. "Get out of that monster's way!"

As Wei ideas went, this struck both Charley and Lizzie as a pretty good one. Indeed, they were about to follow the captain's advice when Lizzie suddenly realized that the silver tabby was no longer in her arms.

"Oh my gosh!" Lizzie finally understood what Mrs Moscos was trying to tell them before the soldier took their sunglasses. "It's a lermin! Charley, that wasn't a tabby cat – and that isn't a dragon! It's a lermin. It's protecting us. That's what Mrs Moscos meant! Come on, Charley, quick! This is our chance!"

Dragging Charley with her, Lizzie made a run for the door.

"I hope Mrs Moscos is waiting!" Charley whispered as the glass door opened and they hurled themselves into the mob of waiting captive creatures.

"And I don't?" asked Lizzie. She pulled the transporter from her bag.

She had already pushed the button before she remembered about counting down from twenty.

Surrounded by families having a weekend of fun and excitement, Lizzie and Charley found themselves walking down the red and white striped gangway of HMS *Park World*, a large sailing ship done up to look like an eighteenth-century galleon. This, obviously, was where everyone else had been when Lizzie and Charley were going to the lake and getting on the wrong boat. There were dozens of people making their way down the gangway, all of them talking about what a great ride it had been. Only Lizzie and Charley said nothing. For once in their lives, they were stunned into silence. Only seconds before, they were aboard the red and blue ship with Mrs Moscos, but now they came back to Earth with a bump. Allie and Gemma were waiting at the dock for them, glowing with anger.

"Why didn't you say you were going on the boat ride?" Allie shouted from the dock. "If we hadn't checked the passenger list we might've thought you'd been kidnapped."

"That's right," put in Gemma. "You almost made us miss lunch!"

"Good grief!" Charley whispered. "I forgot about them."

"Me too," said Lizzie. "But I'm almost glad to see them."

Though not, of course, for long.

Allie and Gemma were taking them back to the hotel.

"We're going to the water show without you," said Allie. "You two can spend the afternoon in your room."

"That's fine," said Lizzie. "We're really tired anyway. We'll probably take a nap."

Gemma went off like the siren on an ambulance, which meant that she found that last statement hysterically funny.

"*You're* tired? From doing what exactly? Sitting in a deckchair?"

Allie started shrieking with laughter too. "What wimps you two are. You're worse than babies. We're the ones who should be tired."

"Tired from what?" demanded Lizzie. "From batting your eyelashes?"

"From saving the world from alien invaders, that's from what," said Gemma. "It happens to be very exhausting."

"You have not," snapped Charley. "We're the ones who—"

Lizzie gave Charley a warning look and cut her off. There was no use in telling Allie and Gemma the truth; they would never believe them.

"You haven't been saving anything," argued Lizzie. "All you've been doing is playing dumb arcade games."

Gemma stuck out her tongue. "And all you've been doing is riding round the lake on a boat like a couple of old women."

"What a pair of dweebles," said Allie. "This whole weekend's been wasted on you two. You might as well have stayed at home. Mrs Moscos next door could've looked after you. She's just about your speed."

Lizzie and Charley exchanged a look.

"You're right," said Lizzie. "I reckon she is."

A Good Weekend Had by All

....

The last thing Lizzie remembered before she and Charley came back to Earth was Mrs Moscos saying that they'd better get back to Park World while she took the rescued creatures to their new homes. Lizzie imagined that this might take some time. For all she knew, Mrs Moscos might be away for weeks, or even months or years, depositing her charges in distant corners of the galaxy.

Mrs Moscos was in her front garden when the Wessons pulled into their drive. She looked up when she heard the car and waved to Mr and Mrs Wesson, but she barely glanced in Lizzie's direction.

Lizzie knew what that meant. It meant that, as usual, Mrs Moscos was going to pretend that nothing had happened, and by the morning Lizzie and Charley would have forgotten that anything had. This time, however, Lizzie was determined that she and Mrs Moscos were going to discuss the adventure on the Wei ship.

As soon as she put her bag in the house, Lizzie went next door to give Mrs Moscos the souvenir she'd brought back from Park World for her.

Mrs Moscos was sitting at the edge of her pond, gazing at something with an affectionate smile on her face.

Lizzie leaned over the hedge. At first she thought that Mrs Moscos was gazing affectionately at the large blue and yellow rock that had appeared in the middle of the pond. But then a thin green tongue suddenly snatched a passing fly from the air. Lizzie looked closer. Something that looked like it might be distantly related to Robbie Stone's chameleon, except that Robbie Stone's chameleon hadn't been such eye-catching shades of yellow and blue, was stretched out on the stone, blending in so perfectly as to be almost invisible.

"What's that, Mrs Moscos?" asked Lizzie.

"It's a tabby cat, of course," said Mrs Moscos. "What does it look like?"

"It looks like some sort of lizard to me." Lizzie stood on her toes for a better look. "But I've never seen one quite like that before."

"That is because it does not come from around here," Mrs Moscos replied. "It is very rare." She looked up at Lizzie with a smile that was far less affectionate than the one she had given the lizard. "And so, Lizzie Wesson, how was your weekend? Did the World of Parks live up to your expectations? Did you have excitement and fun?"

"Park World," Lizzie corrected. "And you know we had excitement and fun. Charley and I helped you rescue the endangered species from Louis Wu's ship."

Mrs Moscos was not only the most peculiar person Lizzie knew, she was also the best actor. "And is that some new attraction?" she asked innocently. "Louis Wu's ship? I do not remember that from the brochure."

"Oh, come on, Mrs Moscos," Lizzie pleaded. "You know what we did. You were with us. Why don't you admit it for once?"

"I am certain I do not know what you are talking about." Mrs Moscos stood up. "I have been here, getting Lermin accustomed to his new home, not gallivanting around the cosmos."

Lizzie was about to ask how Mrs Moscos knew they'd been gallivanting around the cosmos if she'd been on Meteor Drive all the time, but something else that Mrs Moscos said distracted her.

"Lermin?" asked Lizzie. "The lizard's name is Lermin?"

Mrs Moscos leaned over and gave the blue and yellow head a gentle rub. "Do you not think that it suits him?"

"I suppose so." Lizzie was now giving Lermin her undivided attention. She was certain there was something very familiar about his eyes. "I just wondered why you named him Lermin."

"Call it a whim," said Mrs Moscos. She sounded further away than she should.

Lizzie looked up. Mrs Moscos was striding back towards her house.

"Wait a minute, Mrs Moscos!" Lizzie took the photo of her and Charley out of her pocket and waved it in the air. "I brought you a souvenir like I promised."

Mrs Moscos turned back as she opened her front door. "And I thank you very much," she said. "But I think you should keep that souvenir. I already have one."

"But you can't. Charley and I—" Lizzie glanced at the photo she was holding.

This was not the photograph she and Charley took in the machine at Park World when they laughed so much they fell out of the booth. This was a different photograph, one taken from a Wei spaceship. Above their heads was the single word *Digglemop*, and beneath their heads several other words explaining why they were two of the most wanted outlaws in the history of Wei.

When Lizzie looked up again Mrs Moscos was gone.